Nesthäkchen's Teenage Years

Nesthäkchen's Teenage Years

By Else Ury

First English Edition of the German Children's Classic

Translated, introduced, and annotated by Steven Lehrer

SF Tafel Publishers

New York

First SF Tafel International Edition, July 2016

English Translation Copyright © 2016 by Steven Lehrer

All rights reserved under International and Pan-American Copyright Conventions. Published in the United States by SF Tafel, New York

Originally published in Germany as *Nesthäkchens Backfischzeit* by Else Ury, *Meidingers Jugendschriften Verlag*, Berlin, 1919.

This translation first published in trade paper in the United States by SF Tafel, New York, 2016.

Ury, Else, 1877–1943

Steven Lehrer (translator)

Translation of: *Nesthäkchens Backfischzeit*

ISBN-13: 978-1523476800

ISBN-10: 152347680X

Summary: Relates the fictional adventures of Nesthäkchen, a young German girl, just after World War I.

Series: Nesthäkchen ; Bd. 5

Ury, Else, 1877-1943. Nesthäkchen; Bd. 5.

School children--Germany--Fiction.

Girls--Germany--Fiction.

Genre/Form: Adventure stories.

Subjects--Germany--Juvenile fiction.

Nesthäkchen (Fictitious character)--Juvenile fiction.

Library of Congress Control Number: 2016931388

SF Tafel Publishers
30 West 60th Street
New York, New York 10023-7909
http://sftafel.com

Contents

Figures

Introduction

World War I, four terrible years of the worst carnage the world had ever seen, ended with an armistice, November 11, 1918. The Germans laid waste to northern France, although no foreign soldier set foot on German soil. The Hohenzollern monarchy toppled, the Kaiser abdicated, and German society fell into the economic and political turmoil that serves as the backdrop for *Nesthäkachen's Teenage Years*.

The Germans were starving. At the outbreak of war in August 1914, Germany had made no plans to husband supplies. The generals expected to crush the French with a single decisive blow, as they had in 1870. With the failure of their military plan (the Schlieffen plan) all stored food was quickly consumed during the first months of the war. Governmental officials immediately took charge of food distribution. But the British sea blockade and extremely poor harvests brought high prices and rationing. The situation reached crisis proportions in the winter of 1916/17, the so-called "turnip winter." The potato harvest was down by fifty percent, and many people were reduced to eating rutabagas. This unexpected catastrophe decimated the health of the German people, and a shortage of labor, fertilizer, and draft animals reduced the 1917 wheat harvest by half. By summer 1917 Germans were consuming 1,000 calories daily, on average, rather than the 2,280 which public health authorities declared was the minimum necessary. Hunger was most prevalent in the big cities. As war profiteers became rich, 750,000 Germans died of starvation and malnutrition between 1914 and 1918.

The Allies maintained the blockade for eight months after the armistice in November 1918. They restricted food imports into Germany until they forced the Germans to sign the humiliating Treaty of Versailles in June 1919.

When *Nesthäkchen's Teenage Years* begins, just after the armistice, food in Berlin is in short supply. Fifteen-year-old Annemarie Braun, her siblings and friends, barely have enough to eat. Fat is so scarce that Hanne, the Braun family cook, is unable to bake enough pastry for a children's party. Annemarie and her friends make a clumsy foraging trip to the countryside to buy food from farmers.

Revolution is in the air and strikes are widespread. On November 9, 1918, Philip Scheidemann proclaimed the German Republic from a window of the Reichstag (Parliament). Shortly thereafter, Karl Liebknecht, a communist, announced the Free Socialist Republic from the balcony, Portal IV, of the Stadtschloss, former City Palace of the Kaisers. Workers' and soldiers' councils were organizing, modeled on those that formed during the Russian Revolution. In her school, Annemarie agitates for the formation of a student council after rough treatment from a teacher. Power plant and telephone strikes disrupt Annemarie's sixteenth birthday party.

For a girl of Annemarie's social class, having to serve as a domestic would ordinarily be an unimaginable humiliation. But post war upheaval leaves her stuck in Sagan, a Silesian town 200 km SE of Berlin, and to earn money she must work a few days as a nanny for a doctor's family named Lange. The Langes soon realize that Annemarie is an educated girl from a good background, as she knows Latin, does not want to go on the street without a hat, is familiar with famous paintings and has a book by Swedish Nobel Laureate Selma Lagerlöf in her luggage. When Annemarie's identity is revealed, Dr. Lange turns out to be one of her father's medical school classmates from Heidelberg. The Langes treat her like a foster daughter until she returns to Berlin.

Despite the hard times, Else Ury's optimism and sense of humor permeate *Nesthäkchen's Teenage Years*. In Chapter 1, Mrs. Braun, Annemarie's mother, smiles to herself as she listens to her daughter and her friends. There was nothing like being a teenager. All the difficulties of the war years seemed to melt away. Young people were through with the evil days. To them belonged the future, hopefully a better one.

Mrs. Braun's hopes give a modern reader chills. Tragically, the future was infinitely darker than Else Ury or anyone else could imagine.

A note on translation: Else Ury liked to write accents and dialects. Vera, Annemarie's schoolmate, speaks heavily Polish-accented German. Hanne, the Braun family cook, Piefke, the school custodian, Hirsekorn, the Konditorei proprietor, and other Berliners speak Berlinisch, the Berlin dialect. Almost all of Else Ury's accents and dialects are rendered here in standard English.

Chapter 1.
The Merry Half-Dozen

The wind howled in the oven. It moaned and groaned. With bony hand it whirled into the chimney, blowing the coals this way and that. The shaking window panes jangled angrily. Like a street urchin, the wind threw shards of ice against the glass. Then it took to its heels. Behind the white-flecked barrier a rosy-cheeked blond head with blue eyes stared out in abject confusion.

"Brrr—it's dogs' weather." Dr. Braun's Nesthäkchen shuddered. How can the girls come through the hail to my party without getting sick? My goodness, they're not made of marzipan, especially Margot Thielen. But she lives on the same floor and doesn't need to get one foot wet. If only Vera's aunt doesn't object. Whenever Vera coughs, her aunt thinks she has pneumonia. Heavens! The world is completely out of joint.

A new burst of hail pounded the window. The white grains hopped and jumped high into the air, as though they were recoiling from Nesthäkchen's nose that was pressed against the pane.

It was cozy inside. A purple satin and silk veil muted an electric lamp that threw its light over a petite coffee table in front of a colorful sofa. Annemarie had pleadingly promised her mother that no coffee stain would tarnish the gold yellow tablecloth on which stood six gold-rimmed cups. In the center lay a cake plate covered with tempting pastries. An impolite young hand could easily reach out, grasp a sugar-speckled pastry, and quickly devour it.

At this critical moment Annemarie turned back from the window into the room. She was aghast. Then she flew toward the offender with a desire to tear stolen cake out of his mouth.

"Mommy! That Klaus scarfed my cake! A whole pastry gone. Hanne only baked six. She didn't want to buy more shortening. Oh God, now one of my guests won't have any cake." The screaming Annemarie, despite her nearly sixteen years, waved her fists at her older brother.

Klaus, grinning, raised a wicker chair to shield himself. "Control yourself, Annemarie. The pastry tasted as good to your dear brother as it would have to your party guest. You and Vera share heart and soul. Why can't you share a stomach and split your cake?" he asked serenely.

Klaus had poured oil on Annemarie's flaming temper. "If only it had been a piece of pound cake." Outrage over the stolen pastry overpowered the girl. "You fill my room with your dirty cigarette smoke. I can't open my window on account of the storm." She energetically approached her brother.

"What?" said Klaus. "You girls want to graduate and you can't tolerate a little cigarette smoke? Next time you want to bum a cigarette, I may need to reconsider." He blew a plume of smoke in his sister's pretty face.[1]

Now a war began over the cigarette. Annemarie was supple as a lizard, but Klaus was skillful and nimble. The two scuffled artfully, as they had from an early age. It was more a joke than an acrimonious battle.

The wicker chair fell to the floor. The flower vase on the window sill began to wobble. Annemarie's blond braids, which she wore with a recently tied black silk bow at the back, sprang from their restraining hairpins. Puck, the white dwarf pooch, jumped on one combatant, then the other, as if to demonstrate his neutrality to the two warring parties.

Wham! The gold-rimmed milk pitcher soared upward. A white flood poured over the golden yellow damask tablecloth.

"Mommy! Mommy! That Klaus has---the milk pitcher fell over." Annemarie's truthful nature forced her to accept a role in the contretemps. "Mommy, everything is floating in milk." The teenage girl called for her mother like the Nesthäkchen of childhood.

---

[1] Emil Ury, Else Ury's father, was a tobacco products manufacturer whose business went bankrupt.

Mrs. Braun appeared in the dining room doorway, a slim lady with a youthful face despite early gray hair. "Children, aren't you ashamed? You should be acting like grownups and you're acting like brats. What will your friends think, Lotte, when they see this mess? You've ruined my coffee tablecloth. I knew I shouldn't have let you use it." Reproachfully, Mother looked at the uninviting table.

"Milk won't leave spots. Coffee would have been worse." Klaus always tried to put the best face on things.

As Annemarie struggled to dam the flood of milk with her embroidered handkerchief, the second door to the dining room opened. The maid announced, "Miss Annemarie, Miss Annemarie, Miss Vera has arrived."

A slim young girl, Annemarie's close friend, entered the room. The light ivory-colored skin tone of her tender face formed a delightful contrast to her deep black hair.

"Pooh! Has there been a war here?" Smiling, Vera dissipated the obvious battle scars. Her German betrayed the Polish descent of her mother, although Vera had lived in Germany for several years. Suddenly she noticed Mrs. Braun standing in the opposite doorway.

Blushing, Vera offered the belated greeting that her aunt always recommended. Vera, an orphan, was growing up in her aunt's house.

"Hello, Vera. Now my Lotte can feel shame before you, since she refuses to make peace with Klaus. Outside the war has come to a merciful end. Within our four walls it still rages."[2] Mrs. Braun meant to sound facetious, but everyone could hear the disapproving tone in her words.

Annemarie was truly ashamed. She did not greet her friend as joyously as she otherwise might have. "Hi Verachen, be glad you don't have a brother in Berlin." Sighing, Annemarie set out to gather up her sprung hairpins from the carpet to restore her hairdo. Vera helped her.

"Oh, I do so wish that my brother Stanni lived here in Berlin with my uncle and aunt, even if he made me angry. Czernowitz is so far away, so far." Sadly the girl stared into the distance.

Klaus interjected happily, "Now, Annemarie, you see how other people think about their brothers. We are highly desirable items." Whistling he walked to his room.

---

[2] The armistice ending World War I was signed in the railway carriage of Marshal Ferdinand Foch, the French commander, in the Forest of Compiègne, November 11, 1918.

Annemarie called out after him: "Yes, I miss my dear Hans. I wish he was studying in Berlin, not in Freiburg."

In the meantime, the maid had laid another cloth on the coffee table and brought some order to the room. High time, since a coffee klatsch demands punctuality.

Annemarie moved the jars with her blossoming pink Hyacinths from the window sills to the table, under Vera's admiring gaze.

The doorbell rang at short intervals in succession, one, two, three, four. The two friends listened.

"It could be Father's patients. His consulting hours are not over." Annemarie tensed her feet, ready to hurry for the door. She restrained herself because Father did not want her in the corridor when his patients were arriving.

The four coffee klatsch guests arrived together. The two cousins, Ilse Herrmann and Marlene Ulrich, never came separately. One always went to get the other.

"Hi Annemie, Hi Vera. Pooh! What weather." The two girls brought a fresh breath of winter cold into the cozy room.

"Marianne, you didn't properly clean your feet on the doormat," said the fastidiously tidy Margot Thielen, staring balefully at the black footprints that Marianne's rough boots had left on the light gray carpet.

"No matter, it will dry," said Annemarie indifferently. "Come drink your coffee and warm up."

"I'll sit on the sofa."

"Oh, pastry."

"Have you done your math homework?"

"I haven't taken it out yet."

"Oh, children, don't start talking about the dumb homework. We have plenty of time for that later.

The girls' voices buzzed on merrily.

The maid Minna brought the coffee, but the young hostess had to pour it herself, according to coffee klatsch protocol.

Trying to be generous, Minna had put too much coffee into the pot. Her mistake was compounded by Annemarie's superficial, careless nature. A brown sea of coffee poured onto the tablecloth, soaking the feet of the hyacinths.

The mood of the faithful coffee klatschists was undisturbed. Even when Margot Thielen, the "virtuous sheep," could not restrain herself from opining, "Annemie, your mother is going to have a nice rant."

All wanted a taste of dessert. A dignified competition unfolded during the division of the pastries. No one wanted to eat a whole torte. Everyone deferred to everyone else. So successful were these efforts that some of the leftover torte did end up in Klaus' insatiable stomach. From the next room he had listened to the arguing. First, he generously volunteered to end the dispute by eating the plum filled pancakes so that the peaceful klatsch would not be disturbed.

"You may want to, but nothing will come of your desire, my boy," said Annemarie emphatically. Mrs. Braun, who had just arrived to say hello to the guests, supported her daughter and suggested that the two remaining tortes be divided into three pieces: honest coffee klatsch polity.

"No, you must learn to play *take out the stone*," cried Klaus, "if you want to be students." As a high school boy he had a keen interest in games, especially *take out the stone*.

"Oh yes, but you have to teach us how to play!"

"Come on, Klaus." The girls assailed him from all sides. They were good friends from childhood. Only Annemarie, who best knew her brother, was hesitant: "You must not participate yourself, Klaus, otherwise you will cheat us."

"Then play *take out the stone* without me." The young man shrugged his shoulders indifferently and pretended he wanted to leave the room.

"Stay here."

"You should show us how to play *take out the stone*."

"Of course, you may participate in your turn."

"Annemie was only joking." The girls buzzed like a beehive.

Klaus gave in. He wasn't sensitive. "Look, you make a fist. That signifies a stone. Then spread out your hand so, that signifies a strip of paper. Cross your index and middle fingers to make a scissors."

Six girlish hands, large and small, delicate and frost-red, strove eagerly to imitate the artful high school boy.

"Wonderful, now look, here comes the crux. The stone breaks the scissors, the scissors cuts the paper, and the paper wraps itself around the stone. So, if, for example, I make a stone and Vera makes a scissors, I have won because the stone breaks the scissors. But if Vera, instead of making a scissors, sticks out her hand and makes a piece of paper, she has won, since the paper wraps the stone. *Verstandez vous*?"

"No."

"Not at all."

"Complete mystery."

"Clear as mud, children."

Lively tumult erupted. Annemarie and Marlene were the only ones who understood.

"Female secondary school students are locusts," exclaimed Klaus, less chivalrous than factual. "Try it once. Practice makes perfect, but not all together, two by two." He gave his sister a fraternal caress. She acknowledged with a thump.

"Go! Marlene and Ilse can start, one, two, three, both stones, once again, Marlene scissors, Ilse paper. Who won?

"Marlene."

"No Ilse."

The contestants disagreed.

"None of you would graduate from school this Easter, if it were up to me," teased the incorrigible Klaus. "Obviously Marlene won, because the scissors cuts the paper."

The black braided Marlene joyously extended her hand toward the delicious, sugar-sprinkled pancakes. "I'll give you half, Ilse," she whispered to her blond friend.

"Just a minute, not so fast, Marlene needs to remove the stone from another pancake. Who knows whether she can keep it?" said Klaus.

Easy come, easy go. Marlene, who thought she could always win with a scissors, now realized that a stone could break a scissors. Consequently Margot, who made a fist, reclaimed her pancakes. But even she was not allowed to keep them. Although Marianne Davis got the worst of it, Vera Burkhard called out, radiant with happiness: "Oh, I have the paper that is more, much more, than the stone."

Finally, the contest was between the two close friends, Annemarie and Vera.

"I concede voluntarily, Verachen. I am the hostess. Enjoy the pancakes," announced Annemarie magnanimously.

"Absolutely not. I won't eat unless you do. We'll play one more round."

"One, two, three," said Annemarie, who remained victorious. "No, children, that won't do. I will not eat the pancake. That you can see. We will compete for the second pancake."

"Hold on there. I lay claim. Teacher's salary," trumpeted Klaus.

"Klaus is right."

"He earned his pancakes honestly."

"We had the pleasure of playing the game," the girls cried out laughingly. Only Annemarie objected.

"What nonsense! We two Braun children eat pancake, and our guests can wash their mouths. Mommy, Mommy, we need a referee."

Mother came.

Father, whose consultation hour was over, came too. "So the merry half-dozen are together again? What is all this tumult, children? Seems to me we have enough going on in the rest of the country." Anne Marie's father, a handsome gentleman in his fifties, always described his youngest as his third boy. Since all were almost in high school, they were forced to accept this jocular assessment.

"Daddy, two pancakes are left. Klaus already swiped one. Now he wants another one. And I won one. This is unacceptable. My friends have only received a half pancake each." Annemarie was agitated.

"Hmm. A difficult matter. What a pity I'm a doctor, not a jurist. Only a Solomonic decision can help now. What do you think, Elsbeth?" Dr. Braun winked mischievously at his wife. "Can our Hanne quickly bake us the missing pancakes?"

Mrs. Braun was not impressed with the suggestion. She shook her head. "It's Saturday evening. Hanne is scouring the kitchen. We can not bother her. She will be uncomfortable."

"I know a way out," said Vera.

"What way out do you suggest?" said her friends joyously as they gathered around her.

"We'll give one pancake to Klaus. The other we'll all take bites from until there's none left."

Everyone happily accepted Vera's suggestion, Klaus above all.

"Get a centimeter ruler, Lotte," said Father and Mother, using the childhood nickname.

"Now everyone can bite off a centimeter and a half. The pancake diameter is nine to ten centimeters," teased Dr. Braun.

But nothing was so precise. Amidst laughing and joking the pancake made the rounds.

"Margot only bit off air."

"Ilse didn't get all the filling."

"No licking off the sugar."

One pancake did more to satisfy six mouths than if Hanne had baked a whole bowl of them. At the end, the little that was left went to Puck.

The coffee klatsch atmosphere, above all, was jollier than ever. Mrs. Braun, writing a letter in the next room, smiled to herself. There was nothing like being a teenager. All the difficulties of the past few years seemed to melt away. Young people were through with the evil days. To them belonged the future, hopefully a better one.

In the one-window room next to Annemarie's, Klaus listened to the general jubilation as he labored to translate Aeschylus from the Greek. "Silly geese, chatter, chatter, and here I have to torture myself." A half-contemptuous, half-envious sigh interrupted his intense concentration.

Annemarie's pretty room was also given over to serious work. The "virtuous sheep," Margot Thielen, disrupted the lively atmosphere. "Children, Monday you write Latin conjugations. We need to review."

"Heavens, does somebody have a gun? I have totally sweated Latin conjugation. Virtuous Sheep needs to remind us, even though she is not involved."

Margot Thielen was the only one of the six friends not entering the Schubert Lyceum High School. Her skills were mainly limited to female activities. Although she was hard working and conscientious, she was not as intellectually gifted as, for example, Annemarie, who was always above her in school.

"Very good, Margot, you can be our old Professor Herwig. You must sound hoarse and cough. Every so often take a pinch of snuff." Doctor's Nesthäkchen formed one hand into a snuff box and with the other inserted an imaginary pinch into her contorted nose.

"Fantastic!"

"Just like Herwig!"

"Amazingly similar!"

Everyone cheered.

"If we do not want to repeat the exam, it's really high time," interrupted Marlene Ulrich, a conscientious, exuberant student. "Annemie, get paper and pencils. Margot, you take the grammar book and dictate lessons 12 to 18, declension, conjugation, vocabulary and phrases, at random. That's the best exercise."

The merry half-dozen sat with poised pencils before their empty sheets. But one of the girls became less merry.

"Not so fast, Margot. Who will help you?" exclaimed Ilse.

Marianne was dubious, too. "You don't know any Latin. We'll need to shake it out of your sleeve."

"Please repeat the last sentence once more. I didn't understand you." Vera's pale cheeks reddened.

"Conjugation, Margot. Herwig will blast us with conjugation. What do you know about the ablative? You're too dumb," said Doctor's Nesthäkchen ingenuously and without sarcasm.

Miss Margot was sensitive. "Learn your Latin alone if you think I'm too dumb." Her eyes filled with tears as she slammed the grammar book shut.

"Margot darling, I didn't mean to hurt your feelings," said Annemarie with happy face. "Don't be a frog. Keep dictating."

"How snide you are to me, how condescending. If you hadn't become so friendly with Vera Burkhard, you'd treat me much better. I can't help it that I'm not going to pre-college classes with you." Margot was filled with self-pity. A handkerchief with a pink border appeared.

"Oh, Margot, how can you believe such a thing? Annemarie loves you as much as me. We're all sisters—coffee klatsch sisters," said Vera tenderly.

"Anyone who takes offense at Annemarie doesn't have much sense. All of us know that she shoots off her mouth without thinking."

Annemarie defended herself vigorously. "Be quiet, Ilse. You often give offense. Now back to our Latin."

Hanne, the old family cook, who had rocked all three Braun offspring in her rough arms, had a different idea. Without further ado she opened the door, put a cold dish, "blubber" the girls called it, in the middle of the table next to the Latin grammar and announced, "Study time is over, now for a bit of food. Take care of your stomach before you take care of your head."

Hanne was unique. She never read anything, yet Doctor Braun respected her. She was totally against Nesthäkchen's pre-college curriculum. It was "pure stupidity" that the child should stuff such mumbo-jumbo into her head.[3]

"Annemarie, put aside all this written nonsense. I want to set down the plate." Hanne still addressed Annemarie like a child, even though the girl was a head taller than she was. But when Hanne spoke of Annemarie to the maid, she always referred to her as "our young lady." That was Hanne.

The pleasant interruption did not anger the teenage girls. They occupied themselves more eagerly with the food than they had with Latin conjugation. They had all done their duty. They had eaten the last crumb of coffee klatsch pastry. If Klaus, a thoughtful boy, had not used up some time, they would have been at a disadvantage. Afterward, it was too late to begin Latin. Despite the recent Armistice and declaration of peace, food remained in short supply. The coffee klatschists would have enjoyed no evening meal.

---

[3] In 1908 German women were first allowed to enroll in universities.

At eight p.m. they had to leave for home. Marlene and Ilse lived far away. The merry half dozen parted after much kissing.

"Goodbye---goodbye, be prepared for Monday." Only Margot, who lived in the same building, stayed a while longer, her pain healed. She was once again Annemarie's best friend.

Chapter 2.
The Middle School Student Shovels Snow

It snowed and snowed, large thick cotton wool flakes, dainty silver starlets, billowing white powder clouds, surprising snow vortices, quiet, steady, even, gentle. A thick white velvet carpet spread over the squares and streets of Berlin. The houses all looked strange with their high white pointed caps. Snow piled in heaps on the flower ledge in front of Nesthäkchen's window. In the morning, Annemarie was hardly able to see her friend Margot across the way.

"A wall of God, a white wall of God! Oh, if only it enclosed our whole house, then I could skip school!" The teenage girl looked doubtfully over her breakfast at the white piles, wondering whether there would ever be that much.

"But Lotte, you're usually not so lazy," said her mother, astonished, as her daughter ate breakfast.

"Today is Monday, always a disgusting day. No other weekday is so dark and cold. And the Latin conjugation exam. If only the wall of God could protect me.

Mrs. Braun laughed. "Lotte, don't be childish. Study hard for the exam so that you won't need to be afraid."

"In school we call it jitters," said Annemarie. "Where are Father and Klaus?" She pointed amazed at the empty table settings. Although Father's medical practice caused him considerable stress, he always strove to take meals with his family. Wasn't this the only quiet hour afforded the busy doctor?

"If you only knew what the two were doing," said Mother with a mischievous grin. "They are making sure no wall of God surrounds our house to prevent you from taking your conjugation exam."

"What? What do you mean?" Nesthäkchen's round face looked so puzzled that her mother was forced to laugh.

"Are you amazed? At the crack of dawn the caretaker enlisted the tenants to shovel snow. Every healthy person must shovel. Otherwise the authorities will not be able to prevail over the piles of snow. All traffic will come to a halt. Your father had to shovel before his consultation hour. Klaus went with him."

"Father shovels snow?" Nesthäkchen laughed. "This I must see." She hurried to the balcony, where snow covered half the door.

"You stay right here, Lotte. The living room is already getting wet. When you leave for school you can marvel at Father."

"I'm not going to school," announced Annemarie with finality. "I'm as responsible for snow shoveling as Klaus. I'm also a healthy person. Hurrah! They can have the Latin exam without me."

"Not on your life, Miss Lazybones," sounded a voice from the doorway, as Father entered with reddened face. "You can't neglect one duty for the sake of another. I'm beginning my consultations. Klaus is heading for school. We worked hard. The hot coffee will taste wonderful."

"Oh!" cried the disappointed Nesthäkchen, her round face sad. "I've been so looking forward to shoveling snow."

"I'm afraid, if the snow keeps falling, you will need to start shoveling this afternoon, Hanne too," joked Father. With his cup of hot coffee he gestured toward the Kitchen Fairy, who was entering the room.

"Oh yeah, cooking is nothing. Kulicke will be out there with me," said Hanne, referring to the caretaker. "Other people may be crazy enough to shovel snow in front of their houses, not me. I know my duty as cook."

Hanne was enraged that "her Doctor" possessed so little class consciousness that he engaged in snow shoveling. What would his patients think?

"So Hanne, we'll meet this afternoon to shovel snow," teased Annemarie.

"You will go to school. You are angering me to the marrow of my bones," said Hanne as she stomped out and slammed the door.

"Funny old bag," laughed Klaus after her.

Annemarie cast a worried look at the grandfather clock in the corner. Heavens, ten minutes to eight, she must rush to catch Margot, with whom she customarily walked to school. Today Margot would not wait. She slipped her fur cap over her blond hair, pulled on her coat. Did her school briefcase have all her books? Yes, hopefully. No time to check. What else? The most important thing: breakfast.

"Lotte, your tall overshoes, you don't go out in this snowy weather without overshoes," said Mother anxiously.

"I don't have time for them. It's incredibly late," replied Annemarie, ready to rush out the door.

"You put on your overshoes, Annemarie," said Father in a voice that broached no argument. When he used "Annemarie," not "Lotte," he was angry. "You had enough time to start earlier."

Annemarie looked for her overshoes in the boot closet. Heavenly Father, where were they? "Minna, Minna, have you seen my overshoes?"

"No, Miss Annemarie, they must be in the closet."

"They're not there. Oh God! Oh God! What will I do?" Nesthäkchen raced from room to corridor and back. Her darling Puck, who got in the way, received a swift kick and crawled howling into a corner. Annemarie paid him no mind. "My overshoes were stolen. A patient must have taken them," she yammered. "I must get out of here. Klaus is already gone." The latter was definitive proof that school had already begun.

"Annemiechen, here they are. You left them with me in the kitchen yesterday." Hanne brought Miss Disorderly, on the point of flight, the missing overshoes. "I need to clean them. They're quite dirty."

"No harm. I'm must get to school." Annemarie was already on her way through the front door.

"Don't get so excited, child. You'll learn more than enough. If you run around too much you'll become consumptive." Annemarie heard none of this from her faithful Hanne.

She had reached the front steps. Down she raced over the snow-covered stone. The heaps were so high that Annemarie could surmount them only with difficulty. Suddenly she lost her footing, flew down three steps, and plunged full length into the deep snow. Luckily it was soft.

Annemarie had no time to be ashamed. Mr. Thielen, Margot's father, busy shoveling snow, called out to her: "What, Annemarie, you're just now leaving for school? My Margot is almost ready to come home."

Mäxchen Kulicke, a true Berlin monster, the adopted son of the concierge, belted out behind her:

Annemarie, Annmarie

You're making a slipping party

"Darned brat," Annemarie raged to herself, not stopping to brush off the snow. "Just wait, my son, you'll get yours!" She felt she had a role in Mäxchen's upbringing. Years before, when he was an East Prussian refugee orphan, had she not housed him in her doll wagon?

The street looked funny today. People could hardly keep their eyes open in their heavy winter clothes. The electric streetcars weren't running because the tracks were all frozen. The piles of snow were so tall that Annmarie could barely get over them. Even the old lawyer from next door was shoveling snow, as well as the young law student and the fat butcher. Annemarie knew them from her time on her balcony during the summer.

Moving forward was not so easy. A slip followed each step. The knee-length overshoes were heavy and uncomfortable. Should she pull them off and try to get by? Annemarie pondered. No, out of the question. Her parents were confident that she was wearing overshoes. To dispense with them would be dishonest. Despite many trivial faults Annemarie Braun was through and through an honest girl. Besides, it would be difficult to keep her school books and notebooks clean if she packed the wet rubber shoes in her briefcase.

Too late she realized that it would have been better to be tardy. She could have missed the Latin examination, a pleasant possibility foregone. Her first class was German with Miss Neubert, a strict, unpopular disciplinarian.

Holy cannon barrel! (naturally, this expletive came from Klaus) the school clock had almost reached 8:30. A deep, oppressive silence permeated the stairs and hallways. The blaring voices of small girls learning their ABC's sounded out in unison from the lower classes of the lyceum.

Margot Thielen sat behind the ninth grade class door. Did she know that her friend Annemarie was shyly sneaking past?

The women's high school was situated in another wing of the vast red brick building. Annemarie stood before the door marked *middle school class.* She had been running too fast, certainly, hence her silly palpitations. She had no jitters, no fear, of Miss Neubert, not a trace.

"Oops?" Miss Neubert glared through her horn-rimmed glasses–owl eyes, the naughty girls called her—at the glowing red cheeks of the teenage girl who had unexpectedly appeared. "Oops?" she repeated, nothing else. But in her silence was a more cutting rebuke, as though the senior teacher had delivered a stinging reprimand.

"Oh, excuse me, please, Miss Neubert," said Annemarie shyly, "it's snowing cats and dogs out there."

"Is that so?" said the teacher. "Do you have any more hot news?"

The class, which usually laughed at the teacher's jokes, did not giggle now. Owl Eyes looked too angry.

"My father and brother shoveled snow this morning and..." she got no further.

"Do you want to tell us what you had to do with it? Even if you yourself were personally involved, I ask that a secondary school student be punctual. I want no excuses, Annemarie Braun. Go to your place."

Annemarie's face assumed a satisfied expression. She was delighted to get off so easily. "Play for God the fife and drum, she didn't write anything in her class register," she whispered to her neighbor, Ilse Hermann.

The day promised endless pressure for the middle school student. The Latin conjugation examination in the next hour cast its fearsome shadow over the usually cheerful Annemarie. Miss Neubert had scant understanding of the oppressive atmosphere. She was dissatisfied with attention and participation in class. Instructor and instructed both breathed a sigh of relief when the bell rang.

For the middle school students it was nothing but a reprieve. No one wanted to eat the breakfast bread that was habitually devoured during the first recess. Every throat was tight with anxious expectation. Marlene and Ilse had put together their brunette and blond heads as they killingly learned all the wisdom contained in the school's Latin grammar by heart. Vera Burkhard stuffed the conjugations of irregular verbs into her ears with her forefingers. Marianne Davis wrote in the Latin book with her elegant hand, "Sixth Class Work" as a headline.

Annemarie Braun did none of this. What more could she learn during recess? She was not her usual lively self. Strangely silent, she stared out at the falling snow.

Suddenly, she called out through the many voices buzzing Latin vocabulary, verbs and declinations, "Children children, I've got it! I have a splendid idea!"

"What?"

"Tell it."

"Let's hear it!"

They crowded around.

"Herwig is surely stuck in the snow. He lives in Lichter-felde. Or maybe he slipped and fell. It's awfully slippery. Heav-enly if the snow has freed us from this exam."

"Unfortunately, that has not happened," called out a cheerful old man's voice in the midst of the bubbly girlish bab-ble. In their excitement the students had not heard the bell. "Your philanthropic desire is not fulfilled, Braun. Neither the train nor I got stuck in the snow. Hah hah hah!" The old man laughed as he coughed.

He suddenly struck a different tone. "Now take out your examination notebooks."

Notebooks flew onto the black school desks, pens poised. The girls were all ears. Everyone thought her neighbor must hear the loud thumping of her heart.

"First sentence: I hope that Carthage will be defeated soon," dictated Professor Herwig, walking up and down the rows of desks.

Happy girlish faces everywhere: the sentence was not difficult. Pens scratched.

"Is the word *victum?*" whispered Vera, behind the handkerchief she held over her mouth, to her friend Annemarie, who nodded.

Oh, if it only stays this easy."

"Second sentence: When Caesar crossed the Rubicon, he spoke the memorable words..."

"Someone's knocking," yelled the class

"Someone's knocking?" The old man looked blankly over his glasses. "No, he spoke the memorable words: The die is cast."

"Someone is knocking at the door, Professor." No pen moved. Everyone looked toward the door, whence would come their salvation.

"Open it," said the professor to the student sitting closest.

In traipsed the custodian Piefke, his gray rain hood in his hand. "Professor, I must announce that the upper classes are to report for snow shoveling from ten to twelve o'clock and that..."

"Hurrah!"

"Long live Piefke!"

"No, the snow!"

All discipline vanished. The girls were delirious with joy.

"Quiet! I can't hear my own words. What else do you have to say to us, Piefke?"

"The students should immediately report to the courtyard." Piefke smiled mischievously. He was granting freedom to the young things.

"So we must fly, though with heavy hearts. Ha ha ha ha ha!" Professor Herwig was not too old to feel the students' joy. "But in the next Latin class we will continue the examination."

"Oh, that's not so far off."

"Next Thursday."

"Maybe it will still be snowing."

Nimble hands quickly slammed shut the dreaded examination notebooks.

"Put on your coats," cried the thoughtful old man. The girls were ready to storm out.

The other classes were gathered in the courtyard. Miss Hering and Miss Neubert distributed snow shovels and wooden snow brooms.

"Oh, if only my darling Miss Hering will come with us." Annemarie had always loved her first teacher.

Every girl received an implement.

"You are to shovel the train tracks on Lützowplatz. Don't waddle like a flock of geese, march in rows," commanded Miss Neubert.

"Good gracious, Miss Neubert is turning snow shoveling into gym class. If she heads up our column, any pleasure will be doubtful," murmured Annemarie to Vera.

"Better, much better, than the Latin exam," said Vera.

"You speak the truth. Company, forward!"

"Annemarie Braun, you're a big girl. I don't need to remind you that on the street you must conduct yourself in a well-brought up, mannerly way." Miss Neubert walked next to the secondary school students, while Miss Hering accompanied the younger girls. What terrible luck!

Annemarie made a not very well-brought up grimace that no one in the densely falling flakes could fail to perceive.

"Should we cut out, Vera? Nobody will notice. They'll be too busy shoveling snow," suggested Annemarie.

"Oh yes, the whole coffee klatsch." Ilse, who had been listening, was enthusiastic.

"No, we need to help keep the traffic moving," said Marlene sensibly.

"We can do it on our own. Miss Neubert kills all the fun."

"Psst, Annemarie, she hears everything. She's turned toward you," whispered Marianne.

"I don't care. Today she gave it to me for being late."

It was lively in the street. Everywhere people were hard at work shoveling snow. Joking words rang out, laughter erupted when sleds toppled.

"We sled through our Latin exam with Caesar over the Rubicon," laughed Marianne.

"Annemarie looks like Old Fritz with his white pigtail wig," teased Ilse.[4]

"And you look like Professor Herwig. All that's missing is his pince-nez," retorted Annemarie, never at a loss for words.

In the meantime, the girls had reached Lützowplatz, where the work was going on. There they were separated.

---

[4] Frederick the Great (Frederick II, "Old Fritz") King of Prussia from 1740 to 1786; brought Prussia military prestige by winning the War of the Austrian Succession and the Seven Years' War (1712-1786).

"We want to stay together." The coffee klatschists congregated like a flock of chickens, and were able to shovel at the same corner.

Laughing, the young street sweepers went to work. Though wind off the nearby Landwehr Canal was sharp, they kept warm. Their eyes sparkled. Their cheeks glowed as their young arm muscles tensed. They made progress.

"Ilse, don't get so close to me or I'll caress you with my shovel," said Annemarie through the snow piles.

"Annemarie, where are you. I can't see you through the gusts," cried Vera.

"Children, my hands are clammy!" Marianne breathed on her red fingers.

"My feet have turned to pickled ham hocks with sauerkraut," laughed Marlene.

"Here, take my overshoes. My feet are warm enough." It was good that Annemarie had obeyed Mother's wishes.

"No, no way. You'll catch cold."

"Nonsense, doctor blood keeps you warm." Annemarie selflessly pulled off her overshoes and offered them to her girlfriends.

For a while one could hear nothing but the chopping of the shovels, the whisk of the brooms and the howling of the wind. The tracks would have been cleared of snow, had not new flakes continually swirled down from heavy gray clouds.

"Children, this is a Sisyphean task," said Marlene as she paused with thumping heart. "Compared to this, hauling a boulder up a steep mountain is child's play."

"Down again to the plain came bounding that pitiless boulder," said the girls, quoting their Homer.[5]

"I think we should take a break. Sure, work makes life sweet, but the meringue cake in the window at the confectioner would make it even sweeter. How are you fixed for pocket money?" Marianne, with her sweet tooth, looked longingly at the delicious torte behind the glass window where she was shoveling.

"It's only ersatz egg foam whipped cream," said Annemarie contemptuously.

---

[5] Else Ury is quoting from Homer's Odyssey, Book XI: "And I saw Sisyphus in agonising torment trying to roll a huge stone to the top of a hill. He would brace himself, and push it towards the summit with both hands, but just as he was about to heave it over the crest its weight overcame him, and then down again to the plain came bounding that pitiless boulder. He would wrestle again, and lever it back, while the sweat poured from his limbs, and the dust swirled round his head."

"Here's a sweet white meringue that you can lick," said Vera, tossing a snowball into Marianne's half-open mouth.

"Just wait, you'll get an ice cream scoop from me," said Marianne heaving back a snowball.

A lively snowball battle broke out. The balls whizzed amidst laughter, shrieking and hooting.

"What's going on here? Aren't you ashamed to behave so badly? Who threw that snowball?" From the thick snow heaps a snowman with angry face emerged. A closer look revealed Miss Neubert wearing a sharply tilted fur beret, which had been hit by a snowball.

The girls in their exuberance giggled furtively. None answered.

"Naturally Annemarie Braun is in the middle of all this. I can guess who the instigator was."

"How do you know it was me?" replied Annemarie with a sense of injustice.

The agitated snowman ignored the question. "You were ordered to shovel snow, not to engage in stupidity. Get back to work, no more childish nonsense." The perilously tilted fur beret nodded angrily at Miss Neubert's reproving words.

Figure 1. Marianne, with her sweet tooth, looked longingly at the delicious torte behind the glass window where she was shoveling.

Unnoticed, the corpulent pastry chef had come to the door of his shop. Snow white as his surroundings he watched smilingly the cheerful activity. He heard the teacher's sermon, as well. The fresh young things, who had been overjoyed, now hung their heads like water-soaked poodles. The good man felt profound sorrow.

"Dear young ladies, because you have so beautifully swept away the snow in front of my shop, I invite you in for a cup of hot chocolate, so that you will feel a bit of inner warming." He addressed his words to Annemarie Braun, in order to comfort her after the censure of her teacher.

"Famous!" The lovely face beamed with enthusiasm.

"Bring your two girlfriends with you." The worthy man rejoiced over the girls' undisguised happiness.

"Oh, Mr. Pastry Chef, we are five coffee klatsch sisters. Please, please allow all of us to come in. We'll share our chocolate with our friends." So earnest did Annemarie sound, with her unforgettable, beseeching blue eyes, that the Confectioner nodded sympathetically.

"I know, I know. The family must stay together. Come in, come in."

"Annemarie, what will Miss Neubert say? Shouldn't we ask her permission?" suggested Marlene in a low voice. Although the chocolate was tempting, duty called.

"Your exaggerated honesty sets my teeth on edge," shouted Annemarie. "We can skip permission. That Neubert is way across the street."

"If she sees us drinking chocolate, she'll die of envy," said Marianne as she licked her chops.

Marlene was overjoyed. She followed the other girls into the shop, even though her conscience pricked her. Her classmates streamed into the women's salon and, invited by the confectioner, seated themselves around a marble table. Five fragrant cups of chocolate soon appeared. The friendly proprietor didn't want anyone to leave with an empty stomach.

"So, young ladies, everyone will have a serving," said their host, placing the meringue torte from the window in the center of the table.

"What? We get this too?" said the unusually wide-eyed Annemarie.

"You won't be able to finish without this," said the confectioner. With a broad smile he cut the torte into five pieces. "This will taste splendid after your exertions, no?"

It tasted divine. The good man didn't need to ask. The eager feasting, the devouring mouths, the grateful young eyes said it all. Even Marlene's conscience had to hide itself amidst such glorious food.

Alas! "The joy of life so pure and rightful is not for mortals to partake." It was about to be spoilt.[6]

None of the happily feasting girls noticed the doorbell. Only when a female voice outside at the front counter asked for a bag of cough drops did the girls lift their heads. Horrified eyes stared. Marlene froze with a morsel in her throat. Oh God, Miss Neubert, in the flesh. Why did no one have a cloak to make herself invisible? If only the evil would pass them by.

Nothing escaped Miss Neubert's gaze. She observed everything, even without her owl eye glasses. As she was about to leave the shop, she cast a glance into the next room and froze when she saw the five girls sitting around the marble table.

Despite her fear, Marlene sat up politely. The others, with palpitating hearts, followed her example. Only Doctor Braun's Nesthäkchen remained sitting quietly with her nose in her cup of chocolate. But acting like an ostrich did her no good.

---

[6] Else Ury is quoting from Friedrich Schiller's ballad, *Der Ring des Polykrates:* "Des Lebens ungemischte Freude Ward keinem Irdischen zuteil."

Figure 2. "So, young ladies, everyone will have a serving," said their host, placing the meringue torte from the window in the center of the table.

Miss Neubert stood in front of them. "Can you please explain to me why, instead of fulfilling your duty, you're secretly spending your pocket money on treats?" she said with a quietly ominous voice.

No answer. Everyone thought somebody else would speak. Finally, Annemarie responded. "We're not spending our pocket money on treats. We were invited in," she said as boldly as possible.

"Invited? By whom?" The teacher was incredulous.

"By me," said the confectioner, who had been listening. "I am Karl August Hirsekorn. I asked the young ladies to have a cup of chocolate, because they did such an admirable job of shoveling snow from my door. And if you would like a cup, I will certainly serve you one." The worldly man believed that he had found the best way to mollify the angry teacher, and to protect his young friends from another furious outburst.

But he didn't know Miss Neubert. She shook her head regally, the fur cap still awkwardly crowning her hair, and commanded the girls with an imperious gesture, "Leave the café immediately. Go right home. We'll deal with this matter in school tomorrow."

She sounded so threatening that Marlene immediately crept out. Ilse, her faithful shadow, of course followed her. Vera and Marianne threw painful farewell glances at the large meringue pie. Only Annemarie had the presence of mind to stuff a piece, despite its egg foam, into her coat pocket. Then she turned politely to the confectioner.

"Mr. Hirsekorn, a million thanks, also on behalf of my friends, for your fine hospitality."

"Well done, Miss, well done. If it snows tomorrow, you can use your shovel to earn another cup of chocolate."

Doctor's Nesthäkchen and her coffee klatsch sisters had appeased their appetites with Confectioner Hirsehorn's chocolate.

Chapter 3.
Doctor's Nesthäkchen Founds a Student Council

"If only Miss Neubert's literature class were over," cried the agitated Ilse, next day.

Marlene Ulrich, to whom Ilse's words were directed, nodded mutely. Filled with trepidation she was unable to speak. The poor girl looked terribly pale. She hardly slept the night before, fearfully awaiting the repercussions of the pastry shop visit. No doubt Miss Neubert would give her a bad grade on the final exam.

Marianne, Vera and Annemarie put their heads together. "Don't be such frightened rabbits, children." Carefree Annemarie bit into her breakfast bread. "What can possibly happen? At worst a reprise of yesterday's thunderclap. That won't bother me a bit. I have the hide of an elephant."

The class' fascination with this sotto voce discussion was brought to an end by the entry of the dreaded teacher. Marlene could hardly rise from her seat on account of her trembling knees. Vera squirmed uncomfortably back and forth in her place.

Miss Neubert, dripping *gravitas*, approached the podium with measured tread. There she stood silently as she stared at the group of girls through her owl eye glasses. Some of the students tried to hide behind the others.

"Dear God, let her pick up her literature book. I don't know much about medieval poets, but they're better than warming up the sauce from yesterday," begged Marianne Davis from within her heart.

"I have a distressing announcement for you students," began Miss Neubert, sounding like nothing that had to do with the literature of the middle ages.

"Where will this lead?" five oppressed, frightened minds asked themselves.

"Students, yesterday five of you were disobedient," Miss Neubert continued. The owl eyes seemed to bore into the five in question, then came to rest on Annemarie's rosy cheeks. "Despite my request that you carry out your duty clearing snow without tomfoolery, I caught you five in a pastry shop. I do not want to talk about the impropriety of students visiting a pastry shop without an adult. Your disobedience alone merits an exemplary punishment." Marlene Ulrich was as white as the embroidered collar on her dress.

Another portentous pause: To the poor things it seemed to last for hours.

"I see myself thus compelled to give five students a written censure and a number three in conduct."

Loud crying interrupted the speech.

Oh, Miss Neubert, dear Miss Neubert!" That was Marianne Davis.

"It won't happen again, certainly not." Ilse Hermann sobbed for God's mercy.

Marlene Ulrich spoke not a word. She bit her lip until it bled, but no sound emerged.

Vera had grasped the full significance of the words. Miss Neubert's not right. She cried because the others were crying.

One girl clenched both hands into fists angrily, and her red mouth blurted outraged words: "Well, that is really strong!"

"Do you have anything to say?" The owl eyes bored into the cheeky teenager.

Annemarie's radiant blue eyes lost none of their force, and were locked with Miss Neubert's. The girl was not about to shut her mouth, although Vera tugged at her imploringly. Annemarie would not howl. But she did not hold back her opinion.

"We did not earn a censure, Miss Neubert," she said in a loud voice that trembled with righteous indignation. "We were not disobedient, because you had not forbidden us to go into the patisserie, nor have we done anything unseemly. The pastry chef wanted to show us gratitude for shoveling snow and take us in from the cold to get something warm. My parents were happy about it and certainly found nothing untoward here." Doctor's Nesthäkchen breathed deeply. So now Miss Neubert knew about it.

The class looked half admiringly, half anxiously, at their bold spokeswoman. Oh, woe, what would happen now? Everyone held her breath.

"Well, that is really strong!" Miss Neubert used, without realizing it, Annemarie's own expression. "You want to make rules for your teacher? Not another word! What your parents say at home, quite properly, does not concern me. I have to ensure that school discipline shall not be infringed. And I do! Done! Where were we last time?"

"At Johann Fischart," came cries from here and there.[7] Today each was on her own. It was not a good time to eat cherries with Miss Neubert.

Done? For Annemarie the matter was far from settled. Defiantly she threw back her blond head. What an injustice, an

---

[7] Johann Fischart (1545-1591) was a poet, satirist and publicist, who wrote The Auspicious Ship from Zurich (Das glückhafte Schiff von Zürich).

outrageous injustice. She would not let it stand, certainly not. She would go to the principal and complain. Or--.

Annemarie frowned, a sign that she was thinking hard. But not about Johann Fischart and his auspicious ship from Zurich, which the teacher described to the class. The whole of her thoughts wandered elsewhere.

Had not Klaus said that in his high school the students formed a student council? Annemarie didn't understand much about it. She only knew that through the student council the students could lodge complaints against their teachers. "Now they won't mess with us," Klaus had boasted.

Father was opposed. "You dumb things do not sit in judgment on your teachers. Did the revolution turn your heads? Next thing you know, infants will sit in judgment on their parents," he responded angrily.[8] Annemarie laughed loudly at this remark and thought Klaus' student councils were stupid.

---

[8] The German Revolution or November Revolution (German: *Novemberrevolution*) was a civil conflict in the German Empire at the end of the First World War that resulted in the replacement of Germany's imperial government with a republic. Workers' and soldiers' councils were organized, modeled on those formed during the Russian Revolution. The revolutionary period lasted from November 1918 until the establishment in August 1919 of a republic that later became known as the Weimar Republic.

Now, in her indignation, Annemarie no longer believed student councils were dumb. On the contrary, they were absolutely necessary to rein in the unlimited power of the teachers. What was possible in Klaus' high school should be possible in her school. She was in the same type of school and no less intelligent than Klaus and his classmates. Why should she and her friends be victimized just because they were girls? Why indeed?

"You, Vera," Annemarie said, poking the ribs of her girlfriend sitting next to her. "I'm founding a student council. Then Miss Neubert will sit up and take notice."

"What?" Vera looked puzzled. She had no idea what Annemarie was talking about.

"I'm founding a student council that will have judiciary authority over Miss Neubert--"

"Vera Burkhard, tell us the content of the poem that was recited." The teacher had noticed that the two girls were not paying attention.

Vera rocketed up from her chair. "Riflemen once sailed on a ship from Zurich to Hamburg." Having Listened to Annemarie, the excited Vera had only heard half. "Rifles are carried. Rifles are carried to the streets of Zurich." Vera's words stuck in the ear of her friend.

Peals of laughter rose in the class. The Polish girl, with her poor German, often made the other students laugh. She had a fetching way of laughing with them.

Today, Vera did not laugh along with the rest. Anxiously she glanced at Miss Neubert's angry face.

"I think, Vera Burkhard, that you would have sufficient grounds to pay doubly as much attention to me. You should use every moment to improve your faulty German. I find it impossible to recommend you for promotion."

Tears began to flow from the scolded Vera. But consolation arrived from nearby. "Don't howl, Vera. You can do more than sit here. My student council will take care of you."

Vera's tears dried up. She envisioned the student council as an earthly version of the Last Judgment before the Lord. Yes, it would be like that.

"Marlene Ulrich, tell us the content of the poem."

The girl seemed to emerge from another world, so engrossed was she in her pain. But she pulled herself together. "In the 16th century riflemen sailed on a ship from Zurich to..." She paused, blushed and lowered her head sheepishly.

"To Strasbourg," added Annemarie in a helpful, sisterly way, though she sat several seats away. Owl Eyes threw her a withering look.

"To Strasbourg," Marlene sighed with relief. "And as a sign that they put off the trip for one day, they brought a kettle of porridge, cooked in Zurich, still warm to Strasbourg," she finished fluently.

"Be Seated!" Miss Neubert made a note in her book. "To what genre of poems belongs the Lucky Ship from Zurich?"

The students were puzzled. A single index finger went up. It was Annemarie Braun's. Doctor's Nesthäkchen had a special interest in German literature. The teacher ignored her.

"Does anyone know?"

"Me. Yes. Me." No one could miss Annemarie's loud voice. Miss Neubert managed to.

"Is it a lyric poem?" she asked.

"No! No!" Annemarie's voice was loudest of all. Her index finger made wild circles in the air.

"Well, what kind?"

"A narrative," Annemarie excitedly screamed, without being asked.

"Here you only speak when I call on you," said Miss Neubert frowning.

"If you don't call on me, all I can do is report I'm present," answered Annemarie rudely.

"Annemarie Braun, I think you want a better acquaintance with the class register for the second time today." The teacher reached for the dangerous book.

"Absolutely not, but I'm not made of air. If I am taking part in instruction…" she said, becoming red with excitement.

"Students, any girl who is disobedient does not exist, as far as I'm concerned. I don't want to hear another word on the matter." In elegant, large letters, Miss Neubert entered a second demerit in her register for Annemarie.

"I'm not at all pleased," said Annemarie. "I'm going to the principal. We're forming school counsels like the one Klaus has organized in his high school. Since the revolution, we don't need to put up with treatment like this. Young people have rights. We're free individuals, not enslaved souls," she raged, as Vera tried in vain to calm her.

"Don't talk so loud. You're flying off the handle."

Annemarie's excitement had lent her equanimity. Not a tear did she shed over her rebuke. Only indignation, boundless indignation, showed in her young, expressive face. Giving no thought to the remainder of the hour, she took a book from her case and flipped it open. If Miss Neubert excluded her from the instruction, fine, she would get hers in spades.

Her companions watched with astonished, disapproving glances the brazen Annemarie. The bold girl had slammed her French book on her desk, opened it, and begun to prepare *Athalie.*[9] Marianne Davis almost wrenched her neck as she turned to take in this spectacle. Vera urgently whispered: "Close the book. Miss Neubert is looking at us with her terrible owl eyes."

Annemarie allowed nothing to disturb her. She did not hear the teacher's lecture about Johann Fischart and his poem, because she had stuffed both index fingers in her ears.

Ilse Hermann, who was sitting in front of her, was called, and anxiously turned her smoothly parted blond head to both sides. A pitying, compassionate soul bore witness to her factitial deafness, and Annemarie paid attention.

"Can you really name us no other work of this narrative poet, Ilse Hermann?"

Ilse was clueless and embarrassed. She put one of her long blond braids in her mouth.

---

[9] Athalie is a 1691 French play, the final tragedy of playwright Jean Racine.

"Flöhhatz," trumpeted suddenly through the stillness. For a moment the girls sat rigidly on account of Annemarie's brazenness. Then the class broke out into loud, restrained laughter.

"Quiet. I demand instant silence." The voice of the teacher mixed icily with the bright girlish laughter. "Annemarie Braun, leave the classroom immediately."

"I've done nothing except name another work by Fischart." Annemarie slammed Racine's play shut with a loud bang. Head held high, she quit the scene of her heroic deeds.

No matter how she may have looked, she didn't feel right. She was humiliated, kicked out of class. Her classmates all witnessed her disgrace.

Annemarie's stomping of her foot on the stone floor hallway echoed loudly through the silence. Tears of rebellion sprang to her hot eyes.

She could not be treated like this. Oh no! Miss Neubert had no right to exclude her from class. Today, she would found a student council that could intercede with the principal. Miss Neubert would not like it.

Miss Hothead would prefer running immediately to the principal to complain of her treatment. But everything must be in order. The students had to move forward together. Only in unity is there strength. Alone, if she lodged an appeal, it was nothing more than the vulgar carping that Annemarie Braun had despised from childhood.

Piefke's bell redeemed Annemarie from her exile. As inconspicuously as possible, she mingled with the other pupils. After Miss Neubert left the class, they immediately stormed the lectern.

"You five are all censured, and Annemarie Braun has a double censure," cried one, the first, grasping the class book amidst deafeningly pitiful sobs.

"Quiet, children! Don't howl like a moonstruck poodle, Marianne. The demerit will be deleted." In vain Annemarie Braun tried to make her voice heard. She jumped quickly onto the teacher's chair.

"Silence!" She screamed into the turmoil with all her lung power. And again: "Silence!"

Verily, the waves of excitement receded. Curious, everyone looked at the young spokeswoman high up on the desk chair.

"Close the door," ordered Doctor's Nesthäkchen. "I have to tell you something important." Even Marianne Davis stopped moaning and pricked up her ears. "This can not go on," announced Annemarie to the attentive girls. "We must not put up with such unworthy treatment any longer. Do you know what we'll do?"

Nobody knew.

"We'll set up a student council!" Like a revelation the pronouncement sounded.

"A what?"

The girls knew no more than before.

"A student council: have you never heard of it?" Doctor's Nesthäkchen felt tremendously superior, yet she had herself learned the expression not long before.

"What's a student council?" A mass of students crowded around the lectern.

"A student council, that's, well, don't you know? A student council is just a student council," continued the young speaker in a clear, loud voice.

Puzzled, her schoolmates stared at her.

"I do not understand," said Marlene Ulrich honestly.

"Well, student councils are set up so that we do not have to put up with abuse from our teachers. We students have our rights, since we are a republic. Have you read anything of the Workers' and Soldiers' Councils in the newspaper? We pupils are something like that." Annemarie was immensely proud of her knowledge.

"How do we establish a student council?" someone asked doubtfully.

Annemarie frowned and thought hard. Such an establishment was a solemn act which had to be nobly begun. "We raise our right hands and recite together the words of the confederates on the Rütli: 'we want to be a united nation of brothers, oh, no, sisters, not separated by distress or danger. '"[10]

The girls found it all exquisitely beautiful and solemn. Only Marlene was hesitant: "If only Miss Neubert doesn't censure us again."

"She can't if we have our student council," triumphantly exclaimed Annemarie. "So raise your hands—your right one, Vera--and repeat after me: We want to be a united nation of sisters, not separated by distress or danger" Loudly, gravely, the oath echoed through the room.

"Oops! Are you performing *Wilhelm Tell* here?" A man's puzzled voice emerged through the doorway, interrupting the

---

[10] The Rütli Oath (*Rütlischwur*) is a legendary oath of the Old Swiss Confederacy, taken on the Rütli, a meadow above Lake Lucerne near Seelisberg. The oath is notably featured in the play William Tell (Wilhelm Tell) by Friedrich Schiller.

famous oath. Professor Möbus entered the classroom for the French hour.

Whiz! The swarm broke up and fled to their seats. Everybody forgot about their oath, and separating in distress or danger. Alone, Doctor's Nesthäkchen remained enthroned on the chair. Annemarie was so taken aback by the sudden entrance of the teacher that she forgot to descend from her perch.

"Oops?" Shaking his head, the professor looked at the frozen statue of a young lady. "Do you want to play the Berolina from Alexanderplatz, Braun?"[11]

Annemarie came back to life. "Nope," she said and leaped down to her place.

The day's French class engaged no one. The student council haunted the blond and brunette girlish heads.

"At midnight we have to come together and take the oath, under the moonlight, otherwise it's not a bit poetic," whispered Ilse Hermann.

"We must all bring sweets tomorrow to the worthy celebration," suggested Marianne. No wonder that the translation

---

[11] Berolina is the female personification of Berlin. One of the best-known representations of Berolina was the statue that once stood in Alexanderplatz. In 1942, it was removed and melted down for war material.

of *Athalie* did not go well. The grades the French teacher wrote in his book were not particularly impressive.

After completion of the hour the girls gathered again around the founder of the student council.

"We must elect a board," suggested one in front, whose father worked in many organizations.

"Yes, of course" "

"Annemarie Braun has to be on the board."

"She should herself select the others."

Everyone shouted to be heard.

"Fine." Annemarie graciously accepted her task. "I select Marlene, Ilse, Vera and Marianne to be on the board." Naturally she chose her coffee klatsch sisters.

"Nah, only your girlfriends, that will not do," came the objection.

"I would not like to be the board," said Marlene. "First I must see how the matter of the censure develops. My mom will be furious."

"Let's go straight to the principal and file a complaint about the unjust censure." Annemarie tried to persuade her friends. But Ilse and Marianne had suddenly lost their desire to join the board. Go to the principal and complain about a teacher? No, that was too risky.

Only Vera, the intimate friend, remained true to the oath not to separate in danger.

"Three members we need at least, otherwise our delegation will not be credible," said Annemarie. "Who else wants to be on the board?"

Embarrassed female faces were eloquently silent. No one felt like making the dangerous visit to the principal.

"You have no spunk; you are not worthy to be high school students. The boys are made of quite different stuff from you," announced the young chairman of the new student council to her comrades.

Finally, one girl volunteered. She was not highly regarded in the class and not particularly well respected by her teachers. Annemarie would rather have had one of the hardest workers, but when in trouble the devil will eat flies, she thought.

"Will you really go to the principal?" The coffee klatsch girlfriends tried again to talk the enterprising Annemarie out of her rash idea.

"Annemarie, we'll fly like the wind to the principal," said Vera softly.

"Whoever is afraid can stay here." Even her bosom buddies were now angry with Annemarie. "The student council of our school expected more support," she said grandly, and left the class with proud head and heart pounding. Vera and the third in the league strolled uneasily behind her.

The closer they came to the principal's door, the slower their steps and the faster the beating of their hearts. For a moment they hesitated, even the saucy Annemarie, before she dared to knock at the door with its daunting frosted glass panes.

A pause.

"Come in," called a voice from inside.

"Aren't we being too hasty?" Vera pulled anxiously backwards.

"Coward!" Although Doctor's Nesthäkchen was by no means in the best mood, she boldly opened the dangerous door.

The principal was sitting at his desk, looking over his spectacles at the three girls modestly standing in his doorway.

"Why, behold, three Graces. What do you beauties bring me?" He asked sympathetically.[12]

The principal's benevolent old eyes caused Annemarie to hesitate in making her angry complaint. Did she truly want to rat out Miss Neubert? Phooey! She could still make nice and smooth out the whole thing.

"Yes?" The principal waited for an answer.

Nothing would help now. She must spill it.

"Miss Neubert gave me and my friends demerits unjustly," said Annemarie, flaming red. For the first time in her life she was informing on someone.

"Unjustly?" The principal's friendly smile vanished.

"Yes, we were shoveling snow. A confectioner, whose doorway we shoveled, rewarded us with a cup of chocolate for our work. And for that Miss Neubert censured us," she blurted out, again quite defiant with indignation.

"Hmm, does not seem very likely, probably another side to the story. And what do you and your two friends want with me?" His penetrating eyes looked over his spectacles.

---

[12] In Greek mythology, a *Charis* or Grace is one of three or more minor goddesses of charm, beauty, nature, human creativity, and fertility, together known as the *Charites* or Graces.

Annemarie clenched her fingers. *Inform.* The word echoed in her ear, amidst the deep stillness of the room. But if she said *A,* she was then forced to say *B.*

"Miss Neubert ignored me. When I continued to participate in the lesson, she kicked me out of the room and gave me another demerit." Annemarie spoke softly, overcome with shame.

"These are pretty nice things I'm hearing. Such unpleasantness is not expected in our school. I will find out soon enough in the conference. What do you want now?" The formerly kind-looking eyes were no longer benevolent. The question sounded short and strict.

Annemarie's faltering courage asserted itself forcefully.

"We want to complain about the unfair treatment. We have experienced something we do not like. We students have our rights. We have formed a student council to oppose any injustice." Annemarie herself did not know where she got the courage to utter these energetic words, while Vera tugged at her anxiously to keep quiet.

Over the principal's forehead ominous, heavy storm clouds had gathered. Now the thunder was rolling.

"So, revolution! Revolution in my school! That's nice! A student council, yes? You do not feel ashamed to come to an old man with such a rebellious idea? Haven't we had enough of the revolution outside in this country? And do you know, foolish child, what these student councils want?" Annemarie had never seen the principal so angry.

"Justice," she blurted out with her last molten vestiges of self-consciousness. "Student councils should sit in judgment on the teachers' injustices and..."

"So, you want to pass judgment on your teachers, you young greenhorns! What about your parents at home? Do you want to pass judgement on them, on your upbringing? You are quite thoroughly on the wrong track. Your wisdom is unwisdom. Student councils should be formed for the purpose of improving the relationship between teachers and students, to foster a friendly atmosphere. Student councils should influence your classmates for the better, so that teachers have no need to punish them. Tell me, Annemarie Braun, are you convinced that your behavior today toward Miss Neubert would have been sanctioned by a student council?"

Annemarie stood silently. Rarely was she guilty of not having an answer. No, she had certainly not behaved politely or modestly

"You're silence is the verdict. Now you can go out ashamed of your childish folly." A brief gesture shooed the shamrock in no time out of the room.

Yes, Doctor's Nesthäkchen was deeply ashamed. So much so that she could barely withstand all the prying questions of her classmates.

"The principal is not for student councils. He is too old to grasp modern aspirations." That was all they got out of Annemarie.

Nevermore in her life would she found a similar organization!

Chapter 4.
Final Grades

Easter final grades this year were set for April 9. Oh trick of fate! Doctor's Nesthäkchen quarreled with the higher powers. April 9 was the most important day of her life: her birthday. On this day of radiant light flashing out from the monotonous chain of years, she would receive the dread verdict.

For the first time in her life Annemarie had a case of the so-called *jitters* before the grades were issued. All her friends were convinced that she could not graduate with a double censure.

Heavens, the disgrace! What would Grandma, with her birthday good wishes, say when her favorite did not graduate? Would Annemarie get the ardently desired new watchband for her watch?

What would her parents say?

Father, who worked so tirelessly in his office from early morning until late at night, always exclaimed as he held her with both hands: "Study hard, Lotte, diligently, so that you may soon be my assistant." Annemarie's cherished goal was to be Father's right hand in his clinic.

She was more reluctant to upset Mother. Mrs. Braun, after having been trapped in England for the first year of the war, was not as healthy as before. Her Nesthäkchen pined for her during that year and treated her with unusual tenderness afterward.

Would Annemarie inflict sorrow on her parents by getting held back in the same class for another year? Klaus would understand, since he was always a crab in school. But in front of oldest brother Hans, who was studying economics in Freiburg, she would be mortified. Hans was invariably first in class, and in his letters exhorted his sister to do her best.

Yes, it would be a tearful world in which the Easter grades were distributed on April 9th!

Doctor's Nesthäkchen thought it best on the eve of this portentous day to prepare her parents gently for the worst.

"The transfer to high school is almost more difficult than the final examination," she began at supper as easily as possible.

"Are you kidding?" said Klaus dismissively. "Maybe for us guys with our stiff curriculum, but for you girls it's like any other transfer."

"Does our daughter have an unpleasant surprise in store for us?" said Father.

"Oh no, no. I mean yes, who knows? You should never be too confident of victory," Annemarie answered hastily.

"No, Lotte, excessive modesty has never been one of your faults," said Mother reflectively.

Annemarie was a good student. She was among the best. She never had trouble learning. If her teachers found something wrong with her, her excessive liveliness was to blame. At home her behavior did not always have the strict limitations that school discipline imposed.

With a heavy heart Doctor's Nesthäkchen went to bed on the eve of her sixteenth birthday.

Sleep well, Annemiechen," the cook Hanne said to her, "and be careful what you dream, because what one dreams before her birthday comes to pass."

Oh, if she was able to sleep tonight, what would she dream about? No doubt of censure, of no promotion, of Miss Neubert with her owl eyes, of the misbegotten student council. Despite her usual candor, she was not about to say a thing at home, not given the punishing sermons she would elicit from her parents or the teasing from her brother. They would never learn what an immortal disgrace she had been in school.

No, she certainly would not sleep a wink this night, thought Doctor's Nesthäkchen, as she fell asleep: deep, dreamless sleep until the next morning.

Gray and unfriendly, April 9th blinked through the window, as if he himself was not quite rested. Her head on her pillow, the birthday girl rubbed her fatigued eyes. Was it better not to get up today? But the birthday party in the afternoon, girlfriends and presents. "Oh, I'm a coward!" With that Annemarie jumped into her small red slippers.

Usually, Annemarie's birthday was during the Easter holidays. If Easter fell late, then the birthday table, used until noon, waited for Nesthäkchen until she came home from school. But Mother feared rightly that thoughts of home and gifts would otherwise distract her Lotte. Today was a noon birthday.

A bouquet of spring flowers emblazoned Annemarie's breakfast setting, along with the elaborate cake that Hanne baked for "her child," even during the most difficult years of the war. "For our Nesthäkchen" stood out in its awkward sugar font.

"Hanne, on my seventieth birthday you must bake me a pie," laughed Anne Marie, who felt considerably older than her sixteen years and no longer like a nestling.

"Ah, I will if I'm alive. May our youngest have a long, healthy life!" Affectionately the good Hanne patted the rosy cheeks of her favorite.

Annemarie, otherwise a bright, cheerful birthday girl, struggled to appear reasonably happy. School was like a mountainous load on her young mind. When father took her lovingly in his arms: "Bring us more joy, as you always have, my Lotte," he would not have noticed if she had cried out with tearful eyes.

But Mommy, who knew her child in every aspect, tore at Annemarie's heart: "Let's hope that today's Easter grades bring satisfaction, eh, Lotte?"

The daughter silently nodded and turned away quickly.

Aha, what was wrong? Annemarie could eat absolutely nothing this morning, not even cake.

"Graduation fever?" asked Klaus, a proper doctor's son.

Annemarie feigned attacking him.

Outside it did not look much brighter than in the birthday child's soul. The snow, which for weeks had embedded the road in white, had given way to a dirty thaw. *Slop weather* the Berliners called it. Snowflakes mixed with cold rain pouring from low-hanging gray clouds, everything gray. Would the sun not reappear?

Margot Thielen, who walked to school daily with Annemarie, had it good. She had no need to be afraid of not graduating. She was such a zealous and humble student that they gave her a prize.

The coffee klatsch sisters were anxious. Would Miss Neubert include the pastry shop censure on their report cards?

"At least, you have your birthday today, Annemie. The thunderclap will not be too loud at home," Ilse said a bit jealously.

"If that Neubert has spoiled my *Commendable* deportment, I will not come to your party this afternoon," thought Marianne, oppressed. Marlene Ulrich said nothing. No sound came from her anxious lips. She looked pale. Vera held Annemarie's cold hand in hers.

"You'll certainly graduate, Annemarie. Have no fear," Vera consoled softly. Vera's own heart beat no less anxiously than her friend's. Who could know if in the Graduation Conference her faulty German had not been held against her?

Endlessly long the ceremony in the auditorium seemed to the girls: the songs of the students, the speech of the principal, the farewell to the outgoing, the prize distribution. Finally, the teacher of each class came to the pulpit to read the names of the lucky ones who would graduate. Many girls' hearts sank.

They caught their breath. Their eyes read the words "to be or not to be," enunciated by the teachers' lips.

Professor Herwig, the teacher of the coffee klatsch sisters, blew his nose awkwardly before he unfolded a large sheet. He took another pinch from his snuff box, coughed a few times, and began huskily: "From middle school to high school: Arndt, Auerbach, Below..."

"Oh, if only my name began with Z," thought Doctor's Nesthäkchen. The auditorium full of girls, the old professor at the lectern, began to spin before Annemarie's eyes.

"Below, Bock, Braun, Burkhard..." A heavily suppressed sob of joy was audible in the breathless silence. All heads turned to the third row, whence the sob came. But in the fulness of her salvation, the lovely blonde girl, who squeezed the arm of the black-haired girl sitting next to her, saw absolutely nothing.

"Stand up, Vera, both of you and the others, too." The names Davis and Hermann were called out. Only Marlene had a long wait for the name Ulrich. But there was no doubt that she would graduate. She feared the censure.

"I want to give Herwig a kiss of gratitude," whispered Annemarie.

"You're welcome, but Miss Neubert is more deserving," said Vera, overjoyed.

The conduct reports were pending.

"Goodness, those owl eyes are impaling me again." The senior teacher was casting some disturbing glances at Annemarie.

What was still to come was anticlimactic. Graduation was paramount. Professor Herwig gave Annmarie Braun a small dressing down when presenting her diploma. It pained him, he said, to see in the otherwise good conduct report a reprimand. To the amazement of the old gentleman, Annemarie had the opposite reaction. The girl's blue eyes shone with pure joy: just one censure. From the heavens sounded the beat of fife and drum!

The coffee klatsch sisters were happy, too. The pastry shop censure was not mentioned.

"I never thought that Neubert could be so decent," Ilse Hermann called out in a carelessly loud voice.

"Hush!" Marlene, who had regained some color, held her hand to her mouth. "We owe that to your student council, Annemie."

Annemarie blushed. Then she pounded her chest: "It's possible that the principal himself acted on my request." She thought fondly of her student council.

Ugly sleet fell to the ground. But the joyous girlfriends, who left school without their overcoats, did not notice. To Annemarie the whole world had changed. She saw no dirty gray rain anymore, only how funny the splashing drops looked as they hit the asphalt. Within herself she was similarly hopping and jumping.

"I do not know, Annemie, how you can be so happy, when you got a demerit on your report card," marveled Marlene.

"Oh, one is nothing." Annemarie laughed at her.

"Write it off as the pastry shop censure; it is less bad," suggested Ilse.

"You actually don't know what misdeed the censure denotes," said Vera, also willing to admit of some cheating.

"Nope. I won't shade it. I will not deceive Mommy, especially not today. Everyone is trying to be so loving," said Annemarie without hesitation.

"And anyone who deceives on her birthday lies throughout the year," warned Marianne.

Annemarie Braun didn't require this reminder. She was an honest girl through and through, despite her weaknesses.

She got home in one piece. The girls separated after endless kisses and reciprocal kisses. They would meet again at noon. Annemarie ascended the stairs to her home hesitantly.

It was actually stupid that the principal did not record the second censure. She did not like it one bit. But she would gladly spare her mother an unpleasant minute.

"Hanne, I graduated!" Like a whirlwind she rushed through the open door to the kitchen fairy.

"Of course you did, Annemiechen!" She could not impress Hanne.

Mother, by the bay window waiting for her daughter, felt a load off her mind. "Confess, Lotte, what weighed so heavily on you this morning? Was it merely graduation?"

"Yes, graduation and this." Annemarie pointed to the neatly written censure that mother had not yet discovered. "But you do not need to be upset about it, Mommy, because Miss Neubert was rude to me and was herself to blame for my impertinent answer."

"Now, now, Lotte, you deserved the censure because of your cheeky nature. You're sixteen. When will you learn to keep your mouth shut?"

A storm raged within the scolded girl.

"Mommy, it is not worth getting upset, even slightly. Yes, if there were a double censure. We have reason to be grateful and satisfied."

"I disagree, Lotte. Your girlfriends were not censured. They are modest and polite." Mother looked distressed.

"Modest and polite? Yes, maybe Marlene and Vera. But Ilse acts as if butter wouldn't melt in her mouth. Marianne's yap precedes her. Some girls in my class got *thoroughly satisfactory* in behavior. Father always says that one should appear below and not above herself, so that no one is jealous."

"Lotte, I wasn't talking about you." Loud laughter came from the doorway. "I was referring to social conditions. If it's a question of your looking for an example, you have the duty to look upward, toward a better student, and not downward. Let me see your report card. Should I spank you, you rascal?" Father grabbed his youngest, as he liked to do, by the neck, as he did Puck.

"Father, you forget that I'm sixteen." Annemarie stood straight. She was not much shorter than Dr. Braun. "No more *rascal*. No more spanking. I'm a high school student."

"Thunder and lightning, did you actually graduate? I thought that surely, after what you had said, you had flunked.

And 'good' in conduct, what more could you want? Just one censure? Such splendid marks must be rewarded."

Father winked so drolly with one eye that Mother had to laugh again. "You've been waiting for me to give you your birthday presents, no?"

"Yes, of course, for you and for Grandma. She wanted to be here and..."

"Granny is, as always, right on time." Annemarie raced out of the room to open the door for the best of all grandmothers.

"Yes, our youngest is growing up. We will soon have an adult daughter, Elsbeth!" Dr. Braun spoke of his girl with fatherly pride.

'You are acting today exactly as before, Ernst. I am angry because of the censure. You laugh about it. If our girl weren't so fundamentally a good person..."[13]

Grandmother and granddaughter, arm in arm, entered the room. Mrs. Braun broke off her speech and greeted her mother.

---

[13] In Volume 3, Dr. Braun's name is Edmond. The son of Else Ury's younger sister Käthe was Ernst Klaus Heymann.

"Granny has become smaller since last Sunday. I am definitely half a head taller," exclaimed Annemarie, exulting in front of the corner wall mirror.

"I think that you are now grown, Luv," laughed Grandma.

"Gift giving can begin," announced Annemarie. "We don't wait for Klaus. He's never on time."

"Oh yeah?" Klaus had suddenly sneaked up behind her. "I raced to get here for you, you glutton, to give you your almond chocolate that you like to gorge on, and what thanks do I get from the House of Habsburg?"[14]

"Real almond chocolate? Oh, Kläuschen, now we can make peace. I thank you a thousand times." She wanted to give him a kiss on the first, barely visible, hairs of his mustache, but he shook her off.

"Done. I'm not another goodie."

Meanwhile Father had rolled back the wide sliding door that separated the living room from the dining room. A blaze of light radiated from the gift table, covered with white damask cloth. The light threw its golden reflections on the happy blond head bending over the table.

---

[14] The House of Habsburg, or House of Austria, was one of the most important royal houses of Europe. The throne of the Holy Roman Empire was continuously occupied by the Habsburgs between 1438 and 1740.

"Seventeen candles--in these hard times--wasteful," said Grandma hesitantly smiling.

"Ernst wouldn't be happy without the birthday candles. They are more important to him than the cake. He saved his money to buy our Nesthäkchen a Christmas tree."

Annemarie examined her presents.

"Mommy, read me the *Struwwelpeter* and not the Gerhart Hauptmann."[15] Annemarie had stuck her nose into one of the volumes. "I don't need a dance lesson dress. Oh, that's cute." The teenager held up the rosebud decorated muslin dress in front of the mirror. "Fits fine! I had a burning wish for the excerpt from *Die Meistersinger*...Gold patent leather shoes!"[16]

"You seem to be colorblind, Annemie, the patent leather shoes are black." A schoolgirl's logic can sometimes be quite distorted.

---

[15] *Der Struwwelpeter* (1845) (or Shockheaded Peter) is a German children's book by Heinrich Hoffmann. It comprises ten illustrated and rhymed stories, mostly about children. Each has a clear moral that demonstrates the disastrous consequences of misbehavior in an exaggerated way. Gerhart Hauptmann (1862 –1946) was a German dramatist and novelist. He is counted among the most important promoters of literary naturalism, though he integrated other styles into his work as well. He received the Nobel Prize in Literature in 1912.

[16] *Die Meistersinger von Nürnberg* (The Master-Singers of Nuremberg) is a music drama (or opera) in three acts, written and composed by Richard Wagner.

Annemarie ignored her mother. This diminished Mother's gratitude almost by half. Annemarie whispered in her ear: "The next report card will certainly not contain a demerit, Mommy. I want to earn all your love." Her Lotte was still a superb girl, despite all her arrogance. Mother could not be angry.

Father stepped forward with more kisses and expressions of gratitude. After him came Grandma.

"Granny, I thank you from my heart."

"For what?" marveled the old lady. "I've given you nothing, child. In today's difficult times, I thought it better to leave it at that, only good wishes. Do you not share my opinion, Luv?"

"Of course!" This admission, however, came out rather hesitantly. "Then I thank you for your good wishes, Granny. You're quite right. It really is better if you go shopping and spend your money on butter. Old people should not be undernourished, otherwise they're through. Father told me that recently."

Nesthäkchen's happy temperament was hardly disturbed, and had already brushed off the absence of a gift from Grandma.

Grandma laughed so hard that she had tears in her eyes. The others joined in. "Well, then, I'll only invest my money in butter, so that I don't croak. Yes, a doctor's daughter must know."

They all sat down at the table. When Annemarie picked up her napkin, she found a small, oblong box.

"Oops?" She blushed with excitement and looked at everyone in turn.

But her searching look came across clueless faces. No one seemed to have anything to do with the box.

"Open it," urged Klaus, who himself was curious.

Cautiously Annemarie lifted the lid.

"A watch band, a sweet stitched leather strap! That's Granny, even if she doesn't want to admit it."

Grandma's soup bowl was in danger. The noodles in the broth were performing a wild vortex, so impetuous was Annemarie's embrace.

»Child, Luv, you make me embarrassed. We agreed that this time I would give you nothing," said the old lady, resisting the lively expressions of gratitude.

"Yep." Doctor's Nesthäkchen was not so easily fooled. "Oh, Granny, how beautiful it is." Her loving glance caressed the new watchband. "How much butter you could have bought!"

Chapter 5.
Nesthäkchen's Sixteenth Birthday

In the afternoon, the birthday table was piled to overflowing. Each of the coffee klatsch sisters wanted to please Annemarie. Vera, her intimate, had honored Nesthäkchen with her own handiwork, a gorgeous sofa cushion for her room.

"I wish you luck for your whole life, and when you lie on my pillow, you shall think of me kissing you."

"You must improve your German," suggested Margot conscientiously. Margot Thielen was in constant competition with Vera to be Annemarie's best friend. This time she outdid herself. Margot had, with surprising dexterity and scrupulous cleanliness, covered a booklet in pink silk with white leather corners. She embroidered on the lid in white silk, "My favorite poems." Inside on the first page was inscribed, in her elegant, accurate hand, her own verse:

What the poet once composed,
What fills me with bliss,
What's dear to me in all my years,
This booklet will preserve.

"Margot, how touching of you! You did it all by yourself?"

Annemarie did not know what to admire more, Margot's idea or her laborious, successful execution of it.

"Look, children, how clever! You've given me profound joy, Margot Darling!"

A giant kiss confirmed the profound joy.

Margot beamed.

But Mrs. Braun tugged at her daughter's ear: "Take note of this example, Lotte, this industry, this meticulous cleanliness and persistence. Can you learn something from it?"

"Nope," was Annemarie's honest answer. "The white silk cover would have been black after I had finished it. That's why we call Margot our virtuous sheep."

Marlene and Ilse, the inseparable cousins, gave Annemarie an inseparable gift, a volume of Storm.[17]

"We have decided to give you a volume every year until you have the complete works of Storm," said Marlene.

"How old will I be when you give me the last volume?" Annemarie inquired cautiously.

"It's the four volume edition. On your nineteenth birthday, we're done."

---

[17] Hans Theodor Woldsen Storm (14 September 1817 – 4 July 1888), commonly known as Theodor Storm, was a German writer.

"Hopefully, I'll live to get them all. A thousand thanks," laughed the birthday child.

"If we're still friends," said Ilse thoughtfully.

"You seem to have good intentions!"

"Ilse thinks she's like us. She's such a bitch."

"Oh, Ilse is agreeable; we never quarrel" Naturally, that was Marlene who endorsed her second self.

"Where's Marianne? The coffee is cold. Oh, let's start without her."

The girls' longing eyes scanned the succulent table with its delicious cake plates.

"The doorbell."

"Who is it?"

"If there's cake, our Mariannchen will certainly not be late," buzzed the happy girls.

It was not Marianne, but Aunt Albertina with her white poodle locks. She was a lot older than Grandma and wobbled her head and white curls when speaking. Annemarie was her special favorite. She had again worked her industrious fingers for her dearest niece and had made a white purse with embroidered lace. "It will match your white sundresses when you go for a ride on Sunday, Annemiechen," she explained.

"Yes, and for dancing lessons in the winter! Oh, Aunt Albertina, the purse is sweet. Not a bit old-fashioned." Annemarie crushed her dainty aunt in her enthusiasm.

"Why should it be old fashioned?" marveled Aunt Albertina, readjusting her disarranged embroidered dress.

"Well, because you..." Annemarie suddenly stopped and blushed. "Because you're so old," and almost added, "because you yourself are so old fashioned."

She stopped herself. That would have been a bad thank you for Aunt Albertina's loving gift.

The ring cake was almost consumed. The crumb cake was nearing its end. Marianne's round face with its brown crown of braids was missing from the circle of girlfriends.

"I'm going to give her a call to see what's going on!" The birthday girl ran to the telephone. But before the phone connection was completed, a small eternity, Marianne Davis appeared, a bit jaded, embarrassed and a mite tearful.

"What's the matter?"

"Why did you come so late?"

"Oh woe, did something happen?"

"Was it because of the censure?"

A barrage of questions assailed the latecomer.

Marianne shook her head sheepishly. "I was delayed," she stammered.

"We noticed. But why? You've been up to something? "Annemarie was quite curious.

"Leave Marianne in peace. She needs to catch her breath," said Mrs. Braun. "Come, sit down here, child. Lotte, you take care of her."

Marianne did not need to be asked twice. She pounced on the coffee and cake, as if she wanted to sink all her pain into it.

Annemarie queried her again and again, as though she could thus make her tactless questions palatable. Gradually, exhilarated by eating cake, Marianne recovered her diminished courage slightly. When the chocolate cake laughed at her, she laughed back.

"Annemie, I forgot to present your gift. I think doing so is the greatest joy." Marianne judged her girlfriend as she would judge herself, but she was not mistaken. Annemarie, the inveterate nibbler, was pleased with the box of chocolates.

"Thank you for the fine confections." A kiss followed, but immediately afterward Annemarie, the child of nature, held her nose. "Phew, do you smell that? It smells like a singed goose!"

"Oh, you've singed a big hole in your hair. Did you get too close to the stove?" Ilse had sharp eyes.

Around the hole was smooth brown hair. Marianne blushed before the prying eyes whose target she had suddenly become.

"Well, I tell you." Marianne cast a quick look into the next room where the ladies had withdrawn. They were in lively conversation about the crumb cake recipe and heard nothing. "I wanted to have hair as curly as Annemie's. I burned myself with the curling iron."

Loud laughter prevented Marianne from continuing.

"Oh God, this is weird" "

"You have burned out your entire bun"

"Annemarie has naturally curly hair."

The poor Marianne had to endure the jokes.

"You look like a sheared poodle." Vera laughed most.

"Yes, Mommy was terribly angry about it. As punishment I was not to attend your party. Father intervened. That's why I'm here."

The last bite of chocolate cake disappeared behind her fresh lips. Marianne had done her utmost to recount everything.

"I was not supposed to come, either," added Marlene. "My father said there would be more strikes. This time it will be the power plants. Because Ilse went, I was allowed to."

"My uncle says that everything sounds worse before it actually happens," interjected Vera.

"Oh, children, forget the stupid stories of strikes," said Ilse. The blonde Ilse had no idea how soon the silly stories would become reality.

"Yes, we would prefer to play games," suggested Marlene.

"Oh yes, fine. Mommy, Grandma, and Aunt Albertina must also play"

The whole group rushed into the next room. Even Klaus, who ordinarily felt it beneath his dignity to participate in girlish games, appeared on the scene. The boisterous laughter drew him out.

They played "tea kettle." Two of the company chose a word that had different meanings. Then they had to sit in the middle of a circle on the carpet and talk about the word, always saying "my tea kettle," instead of the word in question. Whoever guessed the word was not allowed to say it, but had to sit down and also say "tea kettle," until everyone sat on the floor, and had a lot to laugh about.[18]

---

[18] This game is based upon words which have the same pronunciation, but different meanings, as:
Break; brake (a type of fern); brake (part of a motor).
Sew; so: sow.
Leak, leek.
Bear (the animal); bear (to support); bare.
Bored; board (a plank); board (to get on a boat); board (food).
Rent (to hire); rent (to tear).
With the Victim out of the room, the others choose a group of two or more such words and incorporate them in a sentence. When the Victim returns, the Leader repeats the sentence, using the word tea kettle instead of the chosen words. Thus, instead of saying "If I went to board with Mrs. Smith, I would be dreadfully bored by her guests, and could never stand that ugly board floor in the dining room," the Leader would say, "If I went to tea kettle with Mrs. Smith, I would be dreadfully tea kettle by her guests, and could never stand that ugly tea kettle floor in the dining room." The Victim is given about two minutes in which to guess the words, and score 1, or to fail. Then another Victim is chosen. The players may be divided into two teams. One team then goes out, while the other selects. The one who guesses correctly wins for his team; then the other team goes out. Or all the players may speak to the Victim, using the word tea-kettle instead of the chosen words. Or the

Margot and Anne Marie had taken the word *Atlas*.

"My tea kettle crackles."

"My tea kettle is high up in the sky."

"Mine is used in school."

Shucks, Marlene was already seated by the two in the middle as she said, "my tea kettle has now become very expensive."

"Mine is covered with snow."

"I've got it," exclaimed Aunt Albertina, brimming with joy as her poodle curls began to swing back and forth like bells.

"I've got it, it's..."

"Don't say it. Don't. You must sit down, Aunt Albertina," interrupted Annemarie excitedly.

"Sit on the floor? No, my child, for that I'm too stiff," objected the old aunt. "I think your mother is a very clean housewife, but I would not like putting my good black silk on the rug." The poodle curls shook vigorously.

Victim may select the words and come in and pronounce the tea kettle sentence. The player who guesses the words first is the next Victim.

Her shaking curls did not help her when faced with Anne-marie's pleading. "Whoever plays must sit on the floor. Aunt Albertina, we'll put a pillow under your black silk. It's cozy down here. Come on."

Amidst laughter a cushion was fetched. Klaus pushed it into the underworld, below the black silk, all difficulties notwithstanding.

"It's not comfortable sitting here like this," Aunt Albertina said, with a longing glance at her former chair.

"You have to say something, Aunt Albertina. How's your tea kettle?"

"My tea kettle is music and dancing."

"Music and dancing? That's not true."

"But, but."

"Auntie says Atlas but means her satin ball gown," whispered Annemarie in Marlene's ear. "How's your tea kettle doing, Auntie?"

"It jumps; it's round and is a popular children's toy."

"Nope, that's not right, and some children's toys..." The three girlfriends on the floor looked at each other dumbfounded.

"Tell me softly, Aunt Albertina, what word you are thinking of," demanded Annemarie.

Aunt Albertina bowed her head toward her favorite niece, her poodle locks touching Annemarie's rosy ears, and softly whispered "Ball."

"Wrong, all wrong."

"Albert Albertina must go back to her chair." Loud commotion arose.

"Oh, let me stay down here, children," said the old lady, who loved the law of inertia, and had set up her pillow quite comfortably. "I'll need to get up soon and travel home."

"That's impossible."

"Not permitted."

"Only those who have guessed the word may sit down," zealously rang out the rebuke from all sides.

Poor Aunt Albertina! What a heavy piece of work. She must return to her place that she occupied before her journey down to the floor. Two children had to take her by the hand, two more had to help from behind, to gradually raise the stiff boned auntie back on her feet. The children laughed and giggled.

The floor filled gradually; one contestant after another meandered down, even Grandma, to Annemarie's delight. Grandma, never a spoilsport, knew how to be young with the young people. Only Aunt Albertina and Vera remained en-throned, high up, alone. The latter, who had not yet mastered the German language, was not able to guess the different meanings of the same word.

"My tea kettle is being made into a wedding dress," said Mother, who wanted to make it easier for both.

"Oh, now they'll get it. You can't make the game so easy," raged the daughter.

Aunt Albertina had the answer. "But I'm not sitting on the floor again," she exclaimed.

"You must play by the rules. Only the last player can stay up. Come on, your pillow is free."

Good old Auntie could not refuse her favorite. The second edition followed. Many helpful hands stowed Aunt Albertina once again on her pillow.

"Half drawn by her he glided in," quoted Grandma, who was as amused as the young girls.[19]

---

[19] The quotation is from Johann Wolfgang von Goethe's poem, Der Fischer (the Fisherman): "Halb zog sie ihn, halb sank er hin." Germans love to quote Goethe. "Things go better with Goethe," the German

"So Vera, concentrate. What's the answer?" Annemarie hurt her bosom friend's feelings. "You will not need my tea kettle in geography class."

"Seydlitz."[20]

"Nonsense, I do not mean the geography book. What else do you need in geography? "

"The map." Vera was amused.

"Man alive, it's gloomy in your head," abruptly Annemarie halted.

"Oops?" said everyone.

Suddenly it was not just "gloomy" in Vera's head but in the room. The electric light that shone down gently from the ceiling was extinguished.

"A short circuit."

"Something wrong with the line."

"Father will fix it."

---

novelist Martin Walser wrote in the New York Times (March 2, 1986). "In short it's Goethe everywhere, day in, day out. Obviously, we could say any of this on our own account, but we prefer to have him say it for us. Like a necktie, he is our most important accessory."
[20] E. Von Seydlitz: Geographie was a school text.

Boisterous laughter issued from the floor, where the whole company was sitting in the dark.

"You, Margot, is that you?"

"Who is pushing me?"

"Oh, children, I am deathly afraid of the dark."

"Oh, Klaus is pinching me."

The girls were excited. They regarded the power failure as fun. But soon it became serious.

"Oh, I should have stayed in my chair," wailed Aunt Albertina.

Grandma joked, "Children, I can't find my legs."

"Everyone is looking for her legs." Amidst grabbing and giggling, shrieks of delight emerged from a tangle of legs and hands.

"Call Father, Klaus," ordered Mother.

Doctor Braun's voice sounded from the doorway: "Children, what are you doing in the dark? I can't penetrate it even with my voice. The electric light seems to have failed in the whole house. I have a patient in front to examine. I can not possibly leave him lying there in the dark. You've got to take care of the lighting, Elsbeth. Somewhere we still have a military carbide lamp from the war."

There was a burst of laughter from the boisterous girls, who found it funny that a patient had to lie in the dark on the examining table.

Hanne shouted angrily from the kitchen: "Gracious lady, I'm in the middle of making herring salad. What a mess."

The diminutive house maid cried fearfully: "The arrival of darkness is the beginning of the end of the world."

Aunt Albertina lamented: "If only I were sitting on my chair again."

The girls squealed and cheered amidst untold confusion.

Mrs. Braun and her mother tried to break through the confusion with all their energy.

"Quiet, girls, be quiet and help me. Hanne, let your herring salad sit. Light the kitchen lamp, there must be oil in it. Don't whine, Minna, the world does not end so quickly. Find the carbide lamp." Calmly and objectively Mrs. Braun issued her orders.

"I can not see anything. How can I find the carbide lamp when it's pitch dark," cried the maid.

A light flashed in the darkness. Although tiny, it was a light.

"And there was light!" blared the girls' choir from Haydn's *Creation*.

Klaus had the good idea to fetch his pocket flashlight. Like a firefly he flitted from room to room, shining his trembling beam so that father's patient could dress, so that the scolding Hanne could light the kitchen lamp, so that the howling housemaid would calm down, and so that the wailing aunt Albertina could set foot on earth's solid surface.

Before long everything was in perfect order. In Father's room the carbide lamp emitted a powerful smell but no light. In the living room flickered and smoked an old fashioned standard oil lamp, which had long been discarded but Grandmother suddenly recalled in the emergency. In the kitchen Hanne grumbled: "In the fairy lights no one can fix a herring salad." Yet her kitchen light glowed brightest of all.

Gradually everyone calmed down. The flood of excitement subsided. Doctor Braun was working on the electrical main with the assistance of Klaus. The young girls wanted to begin a new parlor game in spite of the lack of light, but were again shaken abruptly from their psychic equanimity.

"The electricity has failed in the whole house. Everything is dark. We should go on strike," Hanne announced in a loud voice.

"So there! I can't work if the current from the power plants is lacking." Dr. Braun rushed to the window. Everyone else followed.

"Then you'll stay with us overnight." Doctor's Nesthäkchen was never at a loss for a way out.

Aunt Albertina's poodle locks shook vigorously. "What are you thinking, child, how am I going to make you an innkeeper? And I must have my usual order."

"We can talk about this," interjected Grandma. "At my place you can sleep well, Albertina. I always have a spare bed. All the relatives stay with me."

"Yeah, and Grandma lives nearby, if you bring Klaus home afterward," agreed Annemarie.

Aunt Albertina didn't like the idea. She had no night clothes, no toothbrush and no curlers. No, it was not possible!

Marlene and Ilse, with their combined strength, pulled the telephone almost to pieces. They rattled the side hooks, tore furiously at the line cord; yes, Ilse bumped the telephone box. But that helped the impatient young ladies not a whit. They got no connection.

Figure 3. A light flashed in the darkness. Although tiny, it was a light.

An amused Doctor Braun, who returned from a visit to a patient in the neighborhood, watched the futile efforts of the two girls.

"Children, you will probably have to wait until the strike at the power plants is at an end. The telephone is also on strike."

The cunning female heads had not taken this fact into account.

"What can we do now, Marlene?" Ilse almost cried with excitement. "Our parents are mighty concerned about us."

Marlene nodded silently. She knew no way out.

"Children, do not lose your heads. You simply remain with us. Vera can sleep with me, Marianne in the dining room, Marlene here in the living room, and Ilse in the consultation room. Ilse must clear out early in the morning; otherwise, it's a fine arrangement." Annemarie offered immediate advice!

"Two can stay with me," said Margot.

"It's settled! We can continue playing quietly. Suggest something!" Annemarie's temperament was light-hearted, despite illuminating oil mist and darkness everywhere.

"Annemie, what are you thinking? We can not stay here and leave our parents in the dark about where we are. We've got to go home." Marlene grabbed her sailor cap.

"You will be picked up, stay calm." Annemarie made an unhappy face. Should her birthday party be discontinued so soon?

"We need to do the laundry. The girl can not come all the way from Charlottenburg tonight." Ilse Hermann would have dearly liked to stay, but reluctantly put her coat on.

"Children, what are you doing?" Mrs. Braun looked sorrowful.

"I'll take Marlene and Ilse home." Klaus could be nice sometimes. "I can take Marianne too, that's not a big detour."

Marianne found Klaus' helpfulness disagreeable, particularly with the herring salad for supper.

"Oh, I will definitely be picked up. I don't live far away," she reassured.

"Tell me, Ernst, will serious medical calls go through?" Mrs. Braun asked her husband. "Perhaps you could notify Marlene or Ilse's parents covertly of the fact that their daughters will be waiting at the light rail station." Mother was uneasy about allowing the two bold girls out in the darkness.

"I can try. Medical discussions are essential, though private traffic is blocked."

"But we haven't been able to get an operator." Marlene was on tenterhooks.

"Maybe they're asleep." When Dr. Braun picked up the phone, he spoke after a wait to the Steinplatz Exchange.

"Medical call to Alexander," he demanded. And when he was connected to the legal office of Marlene's father, he spoke briefly: "Doctor Braun here. I order, please, that the patient Marlene Ulrich, who is currently in my office, be picked up at 9 o'clock from Alexanderplatz station."

The patient Marlene Ulrich laughed like a leprechaun at the successful telephone conversation. Ilse, who lived a few houses away from her cousin, beamed that she could take off her coat. Marianne was happy, too, that she wouldn't burden Klaus.

"My uncle and aunt will come for me," said Vera Burkhard quite unconcerned.

"I hope not; then at least you can sleep with me." Annemarie would have preferred to house the whole coffee klatsch.

They went back to the interrupted game. But the necessary quiet was missing. Someone ran to the window to see whether the lights were on or the streetcars were running. Someone else went to the front door, saying somebody was knocking. Even the doorbell failed.

Supper at the fatigued household was jolly. Why should the happy children care about a serious strike and its drastic consequences for economic life?

The adults were silent and worried. They laughed, chatted and joked in spite of the "fairy lights." Hanne's pickled herring salad garnished with ripe fruit was eaten in the dark along with sandwiches. But Doctor Braun did not have enough food for all. Even a larger weekly ration would not have satisfied the appetites of Klaus and Nesthäkchen.

To Aunt Albertina nothing tasted good. Today she would miss her orderly home. She had to go to bed without her own bed jacket and without curlers. "How can the young girls have been so careless about getting home?" she said, shaking her head and her poodle locks to reaffirm her view.

"The phone! The phone is ringing." The girls shouted, as if this was the greatest wonder of the world! In the Braun home the telephone was never quiet.

"You have no need to get excited, children, it could be a patient."

It was the father of Marianne, a colleague of Dr. Braun, who was as sly as the good doctor. Marianne's father informed her physician that the patient would be picked up.

No one was happier than Marianne. With joy she served herself another fine mountain of herring salad.

The youths were right to be carefree despite Aunt Albertina's shaking of her head. Each of them got home safely. Vera was personally picked up by her aunt and uncle, who were friends of the Braun family.

"Too bad, Lotte, that your birthday was affected by the silly strike," Mother said at bedtime when her youngest thanked her for everything.

"Affected? Don't worry, Mommy. My party was something special. Parlor games and pies are at every birthday party. In the pitch dark we did not have anywhere to sit. We never laughed like we laughed today."

Happy teenage years!

Chapter 6.
Foraging Trip

CHERRY TREES BLOOM IN WERDER was the banner headline in all the papers. Doctor's Nesthäkchen dreamed of the blooming cherry trees day and night.[21]

Annemarie's parents were doubtful.

"Not me, Lotte. I don't want to be crushed to applesauce in the crowded trains." Father laughed at her. "I run around enough during the week. Quietly sitting down with my cigar on the balcony is my best Sunday treat. "

"Mine is not."

"I would hope not. Let's say, instead of the cigar, with a piece of chocolate."

The girl was unmoved. "Sixteen years old and I have never seen the trees blossom. It's a shame," complained Nesthäkchen.

"You need merely to look down into the courtyard," said Klaus. Over the grey-black walls peeked a tiny pink apple blossom branch from a neighboring garden.

---

[21] Werder is a town 60 km SW of Berlin known for its fruit and festivals.

"Sure, you can talk. You've already been to Werder with your friends."

"Lotte, you imagine that it's nicer than it is." Mother was trying to dispel the displeasure of her daughter. "The trains are overcrowded: raucous, jeering crowds. They want more of the dangerous fruit wine than is good for them. When you get there, the cherry blossoms are often old, brown, and ugly instead of snowy white. I speak from experience."

"You see, you have experienced it. You have been there, yet I should not go. Please, please, Mommy, I would like terribly to someday look at the blossoms."

"I'll take you Sunday." Klaus felt his heart softened by the request of his sister. "I'm going with Fritz Richter at the crack of dawn on a foraging trip, not to Werder, but quite close, to Caputh. The blossoms are as beautiful, and Caputh is nowhere near as packed. But if you can not get out of bed, stay home. We will not wait."

"No, no, I'm getting up at three a.m., if need be, Kläuschen. I'll wear my Dirndl peasant dress. The farmers will like that. I'll bring home butter, eggs, hams and bacon. Hurray!" Annemarie spun with joy like a top.

"But Lotte, have we given you permission to go?" objected mother.

"Oh Mommy, dearest, best Mommy, I will bring you a peasant bread." Anne Marie did not know what she was promising.

"Potatoes, they're what we need. The tub is empty, as though they were a delicacy," said Hanne as she passed through the room.

"Yes, of course, potatoes! We'll carry sacks on our backs. At night we can eat potatoes and herring, Father; not merely a scoop of ol 'groats," said Annemarie eagerly.[22]

"If you are referring to my favorite dish, potatoes and herring, Lotte, I must agree absolutely," chuckled Father.

"Hurrah, I'm going on a foraging trip." Nesthäkchen flew, despite her sixteen years, onto father's knee and stroked him gratefully.

"I do not wish you to go, Lotte; you all alone with the two daredevil boys." Mother dampened Annemarie's lively joy.

"I can take Vera or Margot, Mommy." Annemarie was ready to make any concession.

"Why not bring your coffee klatsch? I can drive the whole flock of geese to pasture." At any other time, Klaus' rudeness

---

[22] Groats are the hulled kernels of various cereal grains such as oat, wheat, or rye.

would certainly have given rise to a dispute. Today Annemarie accepted "flock of geese" with a shrug.

"Oh, Kläuschen, do not be so disgusting. Think how merry it would be if the girls all went on the foraging trip. God, it would be simple!"

"Well, hmm," growled Klaus. The thing seemed comprehensible. Such an excursion with the nice girls was tempting. "But if Richter does not want to go with a hotel full of girls, forget it." Was this all getting to be too much?

"Oh, Richter, he is much nicer than you. He would be overjoyed if we came."

Doctor's Nesthäkchen said as usual everything running through her pretty head. Richter would be happy, the coffee klatsch sisters joyous. Parental permission was assured on the grounds that the other girls were likely coming along.

On the eve of the eagerly awaited Sunday, Annemarie prayed with all her heart: "Dear God, let it not rain tomorrow and let me not oversleep."

Before bedtime, all equipment necessary for the foraging trip was ready, especially the gunny sack for potatoes. Without a hundred pounds of potatoes, nobody was allowed to come home, Hanne had said. In addition, a backpack was included for all the other tasty items that were in prospect. Mommy had filled it with goodies as provisions for the morrow. But Mrs. Braun seemed less certain than the hope-filled, joyful youths that their harvest would be lucrative.

Nearby lay a brightly flowered peasant dress, a green apron, and a mandolin, Annemarie's latest accomplishment. In the middle was enthroned the most important element, the alarm clock.

"Good night, forager, do not oversleep," said Dr. Braun as he left his youngest.

Do not oversleep? Hanne had set the alarm clock to 4:45 a.m. The train left at five. If the alarm clock was not working, or if Annemarie didn't hear it because she slept so soundly, her trip was off.

"Miss Annemarie, you must pull three times on your left big toe and say, big toe, big toe, wake me at quarter to five, not before. This trick is better than any alarm clock," the house-maid advised.[23]

Annemarie trusted the alarm clock more than her big toe, but would, just to be sure, do both.

A deafening ring woke Annemarie from restless slumber.

---

[23] An incantation: *Großer Zeh, großer Zeh, weck' mich um viertel fünf, nicht eh'!*

"The telephone, the telephone." Annemarie jumped out of bed to the phone. "Doctor Brown here."

A booming laugh came from behind the door. On the other side, Klaus had been asleep. "You monkey tail; that was the alarm clock. It's time to get up."

"Oh." Annemarie rubbed her sleepy eyes: a rather dubious pleasure, such an early game. Fruit blossoms! But after she bathed her face in cold water, her fatigue was gone and her pleasant anticipation returned.

The stroke of five: A fair-haired, handsome young fellow with sparkling brown eyes, knee pants, a sport shirt, a backpack on his back, and a charming blond girl wearing a Dirndl, emerged from the sleeping house, past the front yard almond tree in its pink Sunday gown.

A moment later there was another thump on the stairs. Tramp, tramp sounded on the quiet street.

"Wait for me, children, take me with you," said Margot Thielen.

"Good morning, it's a glorious Sunday."

"We should be baker boys or milk maids." Nesthäkchen, otherwise a late riser, was suddenly keen about getting up early.

"I wonder if the other girls will be on time."

"The others might, you certainly not, if you drool so much," said Klaus, who strutted ahead with long strides,

They all were on time. Ten minutes before the departure of the train the whole band of foragers was assembled.

"Howdy, Richter, if you put glasses on your nose you'll look like the worthy director of a women's hotel." Annemarie welcomed Klaus' friend happily.

"'Morning, children! Behave like pretty, demure lasses so you don't shame me," said the senior high school boy, returning the joke.

They were immediately all good friends.

"People will think we are migratory birds," said Marianne.

"Then they have no idea of zoology. Any scientifically trained person would see at first glance that we belong to the hamster family."

"Especially Ilse with her dainty new white shoes; on a foraging trip you need rough footwear that can withstand heavy rain."

"And that won't give you bunions."

Ilse turned red. She had fought with her mother over wearing her new white shoes. The vain young lady nearly had to stay home.

"What nonsense, Marianne, that you are wearing your pale blue embroidered dress. That's a disgrace."

"The peasants won't sell you anything if you look so frilly; they will think you have enough already."

Fortunately the noise of the arriving train drowned out Marianne's reply. At home, she had begged Mommy to let her wear her delicately colored Sunday dress. Now that the others, in skirts, blouses or dresses, looked like peasants, she was ashamed.

The train was crowded despite the early hour. But "a packed car does not bother a real Berliner one bit," said a fat man who planted his entire bulk by the open window, no matter that the compartment was already frightfully full.

"Vera, where are you?"

"Here. I couldn't find a seat." Outside the train, she sounded pathetic.

"Girl, sit down here, at worst we can lie in the baggage racks."

"One person cannot claim a saloon car for herself."

"Always room in the parlor." Several hands reached out to help shy Vera into the overfilled train.

"As you can see, Berliners are not potted plants, Vera." Annemarie pulled Vera helpfully to her, though Vera hung out with one leg in the air.

"Richter, is our herd is complete? Off you go, Mr. Stationmaster." Klaus was mighty rude in front of everybody. But not enough of Annemarie's arm was able to reach him. Otherwise he would have received a lesson.

Black pine forests with sparse May growth, dewy meadows, and Sunday-clean houses sped by the rattling train. Annemarie saw them through a tiny opening in the semicircle of the left arm of the stout gentleman at the window. She was so wedged in that she could hardly breathe. The girls leaned against each other to keep from falling. At every jolt they landed on each other, laughing.

It was wonderful.

Annemarie had lost the right to dispose of her legs. One hovered. The other was almost pushed off her. But her hands were free. Despite the narrowness she held her mandolin. Blim, blim she began, "Wandering is the Miller's desire."[24] Immedi-

---

[24] "Das Wandern ist des Müllers lust" is the poet Wilhelm Müller's first line from Franz Schubert's exquisite song cycle, *Die Schöne Müllerin,*

ately, the whole compartment and adjacent compartment were singing along. Soon they arrived at the blue Havel, at Potsdam with its historic towers and domes, and at Caputh.

Outside the train, the passengers tried to reassemble their bones.

"Oh, children, breathe the enchanting air."

"The Blossoms shimmer. White and pink! Oh, that's nice, that's nice." Annemarie enthusiastically took in the snowy sea of blossoms that covered the Havel banks in gentle wavy lines.

Marlene stood still and completely absorbed the spring miracle. Ilse glanced sadly at her right shoe, scuffed black.

"There is more beauty to come," urged Klaus, who had less sense of natural beauty than a spirit of enterprise. "Our main task is foraging. The other Berliners must not slow us down."

"They're almost all gone to Werder."

Caputh was relatively empty. The farmhouses were stirring, despite the early hour. A poor farmer, pipe in mouth, was

---

the Beautiful Maid of the Mill. In Volume 8 of the Nesthäkchen series, *Nesthäkchen's Youngest,* Annemarie's youngest daughter, Ursel, is a talented singer who is allowed to substitute at a major concert for another singer who became ill. Ursel seems to be at the beginning of a splendid career. No doubt she inherited her formidable musical talent from her mother, Annemarie. Singers who can master Schubert Lieder rarely have the ability to accompany themselves, too.

at his front door looking into the clear Sunday sky. A young girl was feeding clucking chickens.

"Hush, child, here there must be eggs, if I ask nicely." Marianne opened the silken purse her mother had given her. She had to bring home two eggs, at minimum.

Richter objected. "No it is still too early. Caputh is on the main drag. We need to forage in the remote villages where few Berliners go." He seemed to understand the process.

So they moved on. The villages were asleep. From time to time a green shutter opened, and a soap-foamy face, being shaved before a mirror, became visible. Among the white lilacs some people drank coffee.

"Eggs, butter, honey and sausages, they have it good," said Marianne, looking through the bushes a mite envious of the rich, heaping breakfast table she was eyeing.

"We'll get everything yet," consoled Annemarie.

"Forward!" Klaus drove his flock.

Delicate white fruit blossoms showered on blonde and brown hair. Stomping through real Brandenburg sand, blossoming youth passed under blossoming cherry trees.

"If they were only ripe!" Ilse seemed to have more sensibility for hunger than for the beauty of nature.

"Where do we eat breakfast?" asked Vera, who had not had time to drink her morning coffee.

"We will breakfast in the first farmhouse." Margot urged Vera on. "They can give us fresh milk for our bread."

"Oh, yes."

"If they'll do it." That was Marlene who stood out as the only doubter.

"Of course they'll do it. We just have to ask nicely," cried Annemarie.

"Now is your chance. Over there is a farm house where they have cows." Richter pointed to an isolated house.

"Don't get thrown out," Klaus cried.

"Me thrown out? I'll bring you a large jug of milk, perhaps even butter and eggs." Annemarie set off full of hope.

"I go with you." Vera hurried after her, a good idea. In front of the house was a large black dog, blinking at the two girls suspiciously.

Although it was Sunday, a woman of neglected appearance rattled around on wooden clogs in the stable.

"Good morning," cried Anne Marie's clear voice through the door.

124

No answer, only the rumble of milk jugs and the rich, comfortable hum of the cows.

The two girls approached.

The tail tassels of cows, moving in circles, were somewhat disturbing, but Annemarie, not in vain, had often been on the Silesian estate of her Uncle Henry. Despite Vera's energetic efforts to pluck her back she ventured further.

The woman had to have seen them. "Good morning," Annemarie said again, her blue eyes sparkling like the lovely Sunday morning.

The woman blinked at Annemarie suspiciously, as had the dog on her doorstep.

"Oh please, would you be so good as to give us some milk," Annemarie asked with all her kindness.

"Nope," was the growled response. Vera tugged vigorously. It was eery in the dim stable with the grumbling woman and her humming quadrupeds.

Doctor's Nesthäkchen could not be fobbed off so quickly.

"Oh, but you have so much." The young girl pointed to the full milk bucket.

"Yeah, we need everything. Not enough for our piglets." The woman looked at Annemarie with outrage, as though she were to blame.

"We're awfully thirsty." Once again Annemarie tried for salvation.

Figure 4. The woman blinked at Annemarie suspiciously, as had the dog on her doorstep.

"Then remain at home and do not drive around the highway. You filthy migratory birds: You break down our house every Sunday! Maybe you want eggs, bacon and butter, huh?"

"Yes, we do."

"Out with you, out!" cried the woman, her voice crackling with rage. Vera had retreated. Behind the barn, she stood and watched anxiously the course of events.

There was not much more to see: a disappointed girl's face, a blowing tail tuft from the stable, and a barking mutt.

Quickly the two girls were back on the highway.

"Where did you put the full milk jugs?" teased Vera.

"With the eggs and the butter?" Now they were even.

Annemarie's mouth had not won the day. "Phew, children, she was one tough broad. She wanted to beat us because we dared to plant our soles on her dusty road. But they're not all like that." Annemarie's happy nature quickly shooed away the threatening cloud that might have darkened their Sunday mood. "Well, Miss Ilse, you can try your luck, since we're in the middle of the village."

"The boys can do more," suggested Ilse uncomfortably.

"Nope, nope, everyone can have a big mouth. Not everyone can do better."

"Marlene must come along."

"Of course, the Inseparables; our foraging can begin in earnest."

"I ask only for butter; fat is the main thing," said Ilse grandiosely.

"Bring in fifty pounds. We will share everything faithfully." Laughing, the group called out behind the two cousins who were slowly advancing.

A bright gabled house behind a blossoming red hawthorn hedge looked promising.

"To me this is very embarrassing, Ilse, as if I were begging." Marlene's shy nature made the job particularly difficult.

"Not at all, we pay. Come on, they will not eat us." Ilse had not finished speaking and screamed loudly her last sentence. A goat bounded toward them with a sad bleat. Ilse's new shoes bounded higher, right into a compost heap. They came out brown.

At the low window stood a farmer, who roared with laughter.

"Well, gorgeous, what do you bring me?"

"Bring?" It was downright appalling to Marlene that she wanted something. Ilse had eyes only for her dirty shoes. Oh, Mother would be angry!

"Do you want something in return?" The farmer smiled. He knew such Sunday guests. The two young girls who dared not open their mouths amused him.

"Oh, if you might have something left over." Marlene would not have been surprised if he had given her a piece of dry bread. Like a beggar girl she appeared before him.

"Do you have any hundred mark notes with you?" The farmer slapped his pockets.

The two girls became even redder

"My parents did not give us that much money," Ilse blurted.

"I have thirty marks with me." Marlene wanted to show that she was not a beggar girl.

"You can't get much with that."

"Excuse me, please." If they were only out of the garden; foraging was horrible.

"You stay right here," said the farmer. "Old Girl, come over here. We have a visit from two pretty young ladies." The farmer's wife, clean and huge, appeared.

"What the heck is this, Pop?"

"We would love some butter." Ilse summoned all her courage.

"I believe it." The farmer laughed again. "Well, Old Girl, we could manage two pounds."

Radiant, triumphant girlish eyes met. Now they could laugh heartily at Annemarie and Vera.

The farmer's wife brought an unimpressive package. "We have ham to sell."

"Yes, yes, ham." Ilse could already taste it.

"We only sell a whole ham."

"That does not matter. We can share it, that is, if it is not too expensive," said Marlene, anxiously standing behind Ilse.

"Five hundred marks, twenty pounds, it's heavy, 23 marks per pound," demanded the farmer.

"What?" The two teenage girls open their mouths in shock.

"No, that won't work; all of us together don't have that much money."

"Then you get no ham."

Ilse made a sad face.

"We still need to pay for the butter, twenty four marks," Marlene pulled out their thirty marks. The butter was not expensive, at least under present conditions. In Berlin you had to pay 22 marks if you bought "under the counter."

She waited for her 6 marks in change. The farmer also waited. "Well?" he said finally, when it was too long for him.

"We still get 6 marks change," suggested Marlene shyly.

"What change do you get? You think this is the land of Cockaigne? 24 marks a pound of butter costs, times two makes 48 marks."[25]

"That's terribly expensive, even in Berlin," objected Ilse with the courage born of despair.

"Why don't you stay in Berlin if it's so cheap there? You think butter grows in the field? A hungry stomach you urbanites always have, but you do not want to shell out." All friendliness was wiped from the hard peasant face.

"Give him eighteen marks, Ilse," whispered Marlene with quivering lips.

_____

[25] Cockaigne is a land of plenty in medieval myth, an imaginary place of extreme luxury and ease where physical comforts and pleasures are always immediately at hand and where the harshness of medieval peasant life does not exist.

"Will you really take the expensive butter?" Ilse quietly responded.

"What's to think about? The butter is purchased, and eighteen marks are still missing, period." The farmer slapped his hand on the table.

Ilse was on the point of tears. She pulled out her purse and withdrew eighteen marks in small denominations, all her foraging money, as she counted out loud.

She could hardly wish the farmer good morning as she retreated with the precious package. Suppressed tears were choking her.

"Bye," cried the farmer, quite comfortably behind her, as if they were parting best friends.

"Such a rip-off!" said Ilse outside as she blew off steam. "I would not have taken the expensive butter." Her courage grew along with her mouth.

"You were the one who wanted to have butter first," objected Marlene.

"Yes, but if it was too expensive, you should have said, no thank you."

"True, but you were standing there, as if you could not count to three and..."

"You conducted the negotiations, not me. Attributing your mistake to someone else is certainly convenient."

"The girls are quite right when they say you are insufferable."

Ilse turned her back on Marlene in silent contempt. For the first time the two inseparables were angry at each other. That came from foraging.

The others had roamed the village in different directions, always two and two. At the church they planned to get back together. Then they would show who had the most success.

Richter was first. "We got hold of a bunch of eggs. And what have you?" As hotel manager he naturally was on familiar terms with his female guests.

"Butter," said Ilse angrily.

"Butter? And you make a face like three rainy days? That's at least one and a half pounds." He weighed the packet on his palm.

"Two pounds," Marlene responded annoyed.

"Children, you fulfilled our highest hopes. You will be added to our foraging federation. That's precious booty."

"Most precious!" responded the two cousins together. Then they looked at each other and laughed. All anger was gone.

Gradually the others returned. Klaus had in one hand a liverwurst, out of which he had taken a few bites, in the other a round brown bread. "Such nice people, didn't want to take any money from me, because I looked like their youngest son who never came back from the war. And we got potatoes, fifty pounds."

"Hanne said there must be a hundred pounds, otherwise it's not worth it."

"Let her kindly button her lip. Fifty pounds was hard enough. We'll pick it up tonight; I left the sack there. What have you got, eh?"

His sister made a despondent face. "Only two eggs, one already is leaking. The woman would have certainly given me a whole basket, but Vera asked with her Polish-accented German, 'How many eggs does the cock lay every day?' You should have seen how the farmer's wife suddenly spread her apron over the eggs. 'For foreigners German chickens don't lay eggs, especially if they can't distinguish between a hen and a cock' she retorted angrily. In vain I told her that Vera's father had been German, and only her mother was Polish. But she insisted on the patriotism of her German chickens."

General laughter followed.

"Vera may not come again."

"Vera must get a muzzle," so it went back and forth.

"If the German chicken will lay me no eggs, I will go to the German pig for ham," laughed Vera.

"Yes, bacon is still missing! The farmers don't want to bring out their bacon, though their smokehouses are full. There is no perfect happiness on earth," philosophized Richter wistfully.

"Look here, a fortune in rose-colored bills." With that Marianne pulled out a pink shimmering side of bacon, which she had kept hidden in Margot's backpack.

"Damn!" The boys broke out in excitement. The girls stood in silent admiration.

"But it cost quite a bit." Margot seemed less enthusiastic.

"Oh, not so much," boasted Marianne. "I gave them my old coat. They wanted clothes. I will mail them a pair of boots, and Margot has to send a woolen dress that is too small for her."

"Thank you."

"That was expensive bacon."

"What will your mother say?"

"You were ripped off."

"The clothes are much more valuable."

The group fell into boundless agitation.

"I did not want to take the bacon. I said we may not give away any garments without permission from our parents. But Marianne wanted the bacon." The brave Margot defended herself with a whine.

"Smoked bacon I eat with relish." Marianne licked her lips with her tongue. "The coat was too tight; anyway bacon is much more valuable." Lovingly her gaze caressed the delicate pink strips.

"Not if you freeze."

"Well, children, we have honestly fulfilled our duty as Berlin foragers. Our backpacks are full, our stomachs empty. I propose that we reward our efforts and have a relaxing breakfast down by the water," said the hungry senior high school boy.

They were all in agreement. The blue Havel shore lay under pink apple blossoms that were more delicate than Marianne's bacon. The band of foragers feasted, dividing their spoils honestly, which was not easy. Seventeen eggs were apportioned to eight foragers, two for each.

"And the brave Schweppermann gets three," said Anne-marie to resolve the difficult question. "Of course, he bowed."[26]

The matter was settled with blades of grass. Marianne drew the longest. "Hurrah!" Marianne became Schweppermann and got, as an added bonus, the cracked, leaking egg.

Less easy to distribute without a scale was the precious butter. Most headaches came from the calculations. How should they divide the bacon, considering what it cost?

"One controls a sleeve, one a button, and the third a boot heel," teased Klaus.

They outdid themselves with funny suggestions. Marianne was allowed to keep her bacon for herself. Margot did not want to give away her clothes.

"We'll get more bacon without having to pay with clothes and shoes," comforted the others.

Was fortune smiling on them? A soldier in field gray happened along the road. The young foragers asked for information about where they could get bacon and butter that was not too expensive. The soldier responded: "In the third village

[26] Seyfried Schweppermann (1257-1337) was a captain in the imperial city of Nuremberg, who bravely led his men to victory at the Battle of Mühldorf. According to legend, the emperor and his retinue had a basket of eggs, which were apportioned, two to each man and three to Schweppermann.

Emit

from here, Hauptstraße 11, lives the cousin of my grandmother. Rike Lehmann is her name. Give her a nice greeting from me, and she should sell you ham, eggs, sausage and bacon quite cheap, everything you want."

Beaming they thanked the apparently brave, selfless man. Klaus shared his last cigarette with him. Then they went on.

It was burning hot on the sunny, dusty road. The backpacks started to become uncomfortable. The foragers walked and walked, but the steeple of the designated village seemed to move further away. Would they give up? No, no, too tempting, what Mrs. Rike Lehmann had for their foragers' greed. Ilse's new shoes began to burn. Vera was totally exhausted and could not continue. Annemarie played her mandolin. The foragers responded with renewed vigor and pushed on.

Finally it was time for Vespers, in the land where milk and honey should have flowed. The village seemed to have only one road. Surely it must be the main street. Where was number eleven? But there was no Hauptstraße 11 in the town. And a Rike Lehmann? Certainly not. The whole village came running to help search.

"No doubt someone played a joke on you," said one of the farmers, who sat in front of the tavern. They laughed heartily at the misinformed Berliners.

What harm that their soles had worn out in vain for glories contemplated? It was a splendid day. What harm that when they got to the nearest train station, they had missed the last passenger train and had to ride a freight train home? That was something new to laugh about.

It was only painful that Ilse's new shoes were black instead of white, that Marianne's pale blue dress had to follow in the golden footsteps of Schweppermann's egg, and that Klaus had to leave his fifty pounds of potatoes in the lurch, because no one was able to make the long journey to retrieve them.

The foraging trip to the cherry blossoms was wonderful withal.

Chapter 7.
Berlin on Wheels

The summer holidays were coming. In school everyone was studying seriously. But thoughts of swimsuits, spiked shoes, backpacks, hammocks and suitcases of all sizes flitted through the minds of students and teachers.

The upper classes of the Schubert Girls' Lyceum were no exception. On the contrary, the coffee klatsch sisters eagerly forged holiday plans. Marlene Ulrich would go to the Baltic Sea and take Ilse Hermann with her. Wasn't that wonderful? The two Inseparables would now be together day and night. Marianne would travel with her parents in the Harz Mountains. "I will need only a short loden cape, no coat." That seemed to Marianne the best part of the trip. She had not forgotten the sermon she received because she gave away her clothes without permission. Vera would accompany her aunt to Bad Kissingen, where they could take the cure. Margot would stay at home because everything was so terribly expensive this year and the family had many children. She consoled herself with the fact that Annemarie Braun would probably not go away. They could go out together every morning for breakfast in the

Grunewald.[27] They would go swimming together at Halensee and sit on the balcony side by side with needlework or books. Actually, it was better than traveling to have Annemarie all to herself, five weeks as her best friend.

A letter upended Margot's plans. The two teenage girls were busy with schoolwork, each on her balcony. Through the thin wall that separated them, they communicated from time to time by knocking in a code they had devised during childhood and practiced as zealously as English and French. A slow rap meant I'm sorry or my work is not going well. A fast rap indicated a joyous mood.

The postman came up the street. Margot did not notice him. Annemarie hurried out to see if he brought news of brother Hans. He was quite nice to interrupt the boring math problems. Before long, Annemarie was drumming both fists, a true jubilee hymn, against the balcony wall.

Margot knocked back once. That meant in translation: "What's wrong?"

The knock lexicon of the two girlfriends was quite rich, but it could not express what Annemarie had in mind, so she sent a

---

[27] Grunewald is a forest located in the western side of Berlin on the east side of the river Havel, mainly in the Grunewald district. At 3,000 hectares (7,400 acres) it is the largest green area in the city of Berlin.

little note on a string fluttering over the balcony wall. It read: "Hurrah! I am invited for a holiday with Uncle Henry and Aunt Kate in Arnsdorf. I'm supposed to help with the harvest."

For a while no response, then three strokes, slow and heavy, came from Margot's balcony. In German: "I am very sad."

Annemarie was terrified. Oh God, she had not thought that Margot would remain alone. Again a note wandered over the vine covered wall.

"Do not be sad, Margotchen. If the railways strike, I can not travel, my father says." Under fiery red geraniums Margot read with eyes a little less hopeless.

"If only a strike would occur," thought Margot fervently. She did not consider, in her disappointment, how childish and immature was her desire: that thousands of people would be harmed and the work of an entire people interrupted so that her trivial wish was satisfied.

Nevertheless, it seemed as if Margot's wish would be fulfilled. Strikes were in the air, even rumors of a general strike.

"What's a general strike?" Margot had inquired of Annemarie over the balcony wall.

"You sly girl, it's quite obvious. The generals will go on strike." Without thinking, Annemarie delivered her explanation.

From Father's room, whose bay windows bordered on the balcony, a hearty laugh resounded that made Annemarie unsure of what she had said.

"Lotte, you're a riot." Father could not calm down. "Your joke, I have to send in your joke."

"What do you mean? It's called a general strike." His youngest defended herself indignantly.

"General is generally. You only have to remember you Latin, high school girl. General strike means—ha ha ha---this is priceless."

"Daddy, don't tell anyone what I said, OK? Not even mom and definitely not Klaus. I am so embarrassed. And if you send it in, it was only a joke, right?" Through the window Annemarie cajoled, stroked and implored her father not to blab about her stupidity. Margot, too, had to pledge silence.

In the joke Annemarie's usual cunning was not in evidence. The joke migrated as an "anecdote" to Freiburg to big brother Hans, who teased his younger sister mildly. Klaus had somehow got wind of it. Probably Margot had not kept the secret, because father kept his word when he promised something.

The coffee klatsch sisters made, from time to time, some embarrassing allusions as to whether there would be a major strike. Everyone kidded until the situation became serious.

One afternoon Father emerged excited during the middle of a full consultation schedule.

"We will do well, Elsbeth, to stock up on food, especially bread. Various workers, my patients, have told me that tonight the general strike will go into force. What times are these!" Dr. Braun went gravely back to his activities, a sea of turmoil foaming behind him.

"Hanne, run to the bakery and pick up as much bread as you can buy. Minna, go to the merchant for our weekly rations. Lotte, you jump around to Grandma and say that she must take precautions. On the way back please bring from the butcher our meat ration. Klaus, ensure that carbide is in the house, if the lighting fails." Mrs. Braun gave her orders, clearly and calmly like a general, yet she was inwardly excited.

But her auxiliary troops whirled around in circles like a startled nation of chickens.

"Oh rats, oh rats, where did I leave the bread coupons?" Hanne tore open all boxes and drawers in the kitchen and rummaged through them in haste. The coupons were in the middle of the table, where she had left them.

Minna lost her head completely. Suddenly, instead of the grocery store, she found herself next door at the barber shop, not knowing what to do there. Klaus made everyone crazy with his carbide lamp; he wanted to hurriedly invent something that would make it smell less. Annemarie was the most sensible. She alarmed Grandmother with her message, but made her carry out the necessary errands. Hanne dashed wildly from one sold-out bakery to another. She dragged home three loaves that she ferreted out, God knows where.

Undaunted, Doctor's Nesthäkchen ran up stairs and down stairs. In the streets, a busy mass tingled like an ant colony. Here, Annemarie met Margot Thielen, there, another girl from school. Everyone was running, buying and dragging, as if starvation threatened. In front of the grocery store a crowd accumulated. When everything was stowed at home, there was new excitement. Margot Thielen drummed up a storm against the balcony wall.

"Annemie, all buckets and vessels that you have must be filled with water. Tell your mother. The waterworks is on strike. In Moabit there's no more water. My aunt's just telephoned."

"Mommy, Hanne, the water is shut off, take in as much water as quickly as possible, otherwise we will die of thirst and can not wash our..." Nesthäkchen was boundlessly excited. She started filling small milk pots, ornaments on the kitchen sill, and crash, one fell and smashed to shards on the stone tiles.

"Twisted wretches," growled Hanne, and ran with all manner of pots, pans and soup terrines to the water spigot, as if there was a fire.

"Above all, fill the bathtub with water, the jars, buckets and decanters—that should do it." Dr. Braun appeared in person to give instructions.

"Lotte, are you not clever? You pulled out the pewter tankard! Fill preferably the basins. That Klaus has nothing but stupidity in his head. He fills all the small liqueur glasses with water. Brat, come out of the kitchen!"

"The confusion was indescribable. Everyone got in everyone else's way.

"This is crazy. They think of nothing but the water shutoff, "muttered Hanne angrily. She could no longer find her way out of the labyrinth of buckets, pots and vessels.

The wily Hanne was wrong this time. When Annemarie wanted to fill the watering can, so that her daisies and tomatoes on the balcony should not suffer hardship—whoosh--it was too late.

In the evening the whole Braun family crawled into bed at sundown. Klaus' invention made the carbide lamp so odorless that, like the gas and electricity, it went on strike and no longer burned. Just as well that this was June and not December.

The next morning, as Annemarie and Margot went to school, the streets had completely changed. No trains were running, neither the electric nor the elevated railway. No cars, no cabs. Everyone bustled about on foot.

School was a mess. Teachers and students who lived in the suburbs and had to rely on rail transportation were missing. Above all, the necessary seriousness and the right assemblage for work were absent.

"We will go on strike. We will not come to school tomorrow. If there is a general strike, we need not work either," a slacker was heard to say.

This proposal was accepted with general enthusiasm, but only by the pupils. Miss Drehmann, who received the resolution in geography class, gave the girls an efficient dressing down. That was the usual designation for such a sermon, whether or not the students were ashamed to wish that the evil resulting from the strike would proliferate among the German people. Everyone has the obligation to work twice as hard at such a time. The young, especially, must strive to bring prostrate Germany back to her feet.

The high school girls renounced magnanimously their intention to strike. But the general strike caused Marlene Ulrich serious concern. She was a sensible girl and worried not only about her own welfare.

But Marlene's birthday celebration was off. She had a steamer trip to the upper Spree planned. She would bring coffee, homemade cakes and supper sandwiches, a real Berlin outing. The coffee klatsch sisters were filled with enthusiasm for weeks. Now the Spree river steamer was on strike. Such rudeness!

"Whether my mother can bake cakes is still questionable. We must stick to our flour and fat allotments," Marlene sadly announced to her no less sad girlfriends.

Annemarie Braun's cheerful nature could not be depressed by such trifles. "Then we'll each bring jam sandwiches with coffee. We will definitely be there, even if we make the long trip back and forth on foot, "she consoled.

But the various parents had a say in the matter. In the blazing heat that boiled the city streets, neither Annemarie nor Marianne nor Vera should traverse the long distance to city center on foot. So it looked as though Marlenchen's birthday party was off, if a miracle did not occur.

The miracle happened.

Not that the strike came to an end. But one morning when the girls went to school, the miracle was in evidence. As though sprung from the Earth; wagons of all sizes, all shapes, otherwise serving various purposes, now with only one purpose: to carry people. What a strange picture, in places a regular barricade. Mankind reverted suddenly from the era of electricity, back a hundred years, to a mess and mass of carriages and horses, exclamations and confusion, cries of coachmen and owners. Among them enthroned was the Berlin People's Wit, laughing and swinging his scepter.

"Here, young woman, you can get to Stettin Station for two marks."

"One place left in my carriage."

"Mother, should I load you in my brake?"[28]

"Fifty pennies for a carriage ride—fast as an airship" the drivers cried.

---

[28] In the 19th century, a brake was a large, four-wheeled carriage-frame with no body, used for breaking in young horses, either singly or in teams of two or four. It has no body parts except for a high seat upon which the driver sits and a small platform for a helper immediately behind. If the passenger seats were made permanent the vehicle might be described as a wagonette.

Annemarie, Margot and Vera were paralyzed with amazement. "Look, people ride in a furniture wagon. They put in benches and chairs. That's funny!"

"They're loading people rather than oxen into the butcher's wagon," Annemarie laughed.

"Oh, the black coal wagons: I do not want to ride in them." Vera shuddered. Yet they were densely filled with people who all had to get someplace in the city and did not want to run.

"Get in, missy, allez oop! With me you ride as cool as the North Pole despite the summer heat," cried a coachman to the three pretty lasses. The wagon carried a sign "North German Ice Factories."

Was it any wonder that they were late for school, given the unusual and amusing street offerings?

Miss Neubert's owl eyes blazed punitively at the latecomers. But the lively Annemarie suddenly broke out in the middle of the hour in heavily restrained jubilation: "Marlene, we'll have your birthday party on a wagon."

No one came home in time for meals. There was too much on the street to see and marvel at.

"The whole of Berlin on wheels," said Father, when Miss Daughter deigned to appear after the soup course. "Your wheels seem to be at rest." He looked angry. Despite his widely dispersed practice he considered mealtime sacred, even with the difficult traffic conditions. But when his youngest described drolly to Mother a striking picture of the scenes in the street, he was soon appeased. A vamp, his Lotte!

The grocery stores reopened, and Mrs. Ulrich could bake birthday cake. Marlene Ulrich's girlfriends took immediate notice.

"Be on time at four; otherwise, the coffee will get cold," asked the birthday girl. This the coffee klatsch promised eagerly.

There was such scorching heat that the Schubert Girls' Lyceum closed its doors by 11 o'clock, and the prospect of hot coffee had to be downright scary.

"I'll put on my white veil dress."

"I'll wear my pale blue; the egg stains are hardly visible."

"I'd like to come in a swimsuit." Of course, that was Annemarie, who had such impossible desires. Nevertheless, she begged her mother to let her wear the brand new muslin dress with the rose buds, which was supposed to be for her dance class in winter.

"It is so wonderfully comfortable in the heat. And Marlene's birthday is a worthy opportunity to inaugurate it. Please,

Mommy, let me wear it." Nesthäkchen had recently become somewhat vain.

"Lotte, you will have no pleasure if you need to be provided continually with a new dress. The wagons you ride in are not too clean. And we might get a thunderstorm. I feel it in my bones."

These three counter-arguments were actually quite obvious, but not for Annemarie. To her the highest pleasure was the new dress. She would look for the finest carriage with red velvet cushions. In her bones lay glorious sunshine.

Half an hour later she said farewell in the rosebud dress. She had begged and cajoled to convince Mother. Mrs. Braun was proud of her pretty daughter, who looked herself like a dewy rosebud. Puck regarded Nesthäkchen with insightful tail wagging.

Phew it was hot! One could see the heat cooking the streets. Every house, every wall exuded heated breath. People crept along exhausted.

The four girlfriends, who met at the Zoo, seemed not to notice the heat. They glowed with the joy of today's birthday party. They didn't observe that the sky was covered with a fine whitish haze. Rain? Impossible!

No one had an umbrella with her, because how would such a black thing look with the delicate bright clothes?

Annemarie's rosebud dress was duly admired, so thoroughly that the only carriage in sight was taken in the meantime.

"Never mind, on to the brake, a lot more fun." Annemarie jumped immediately onto the high wheel of a cute brake carriage, and turned to the driver's seat. That she was wrinkling the fabric of her new dress, the careless Miss did not notice.

"Come on, kids, up here it's got a fine mountain view! Margot, do not be so clumsy, you have to climb onto the spokes. Vera, you'll be doing a full gym workout. Marianne, yuck, you smell like a whole perfume store. How did you embalm yourself like that?" A mill wheel could not compete with Anne Marie's mouth.

They were all aboard. Margot was scarlet with heat and anxiety after the unfamiliar ascent. Marianne was ashamed of her perfume scent. She had gone secretly to Mother's dressing table and poured on too much of a good thing.

"Verachen, we have the best seats." Pridefully the two girl-friends were enthroned, arm in arm, on the box.

"Verachen must get down," said the fat coachman. "That's my seat."

"Oh, we will move closer together; then we will have three places, Mr. Coachman," said Annemarie.

"Nope, when there's this much heat I'm too damp. I'm already sweating like after elder tea. Vera must get down. She can sit in back between the other girlies. She's thin," said the coachman.

Verachen had to begin her perilous descent.

"Oh God, my beautiful dress!" The white veil had grazed the freshly painted spokes and was covered with dark stripes. Vera almost cried with anger.

"We'll wash it at Marlene's."

"It is washable fabric."

"Don't spoil our mood."

From all sides, encouragement came.

"So, Mr. Coachman, now we're ready to go."

"Pay first, two marks apiece."

"Is the third dozen no cheaper?" inquired the exuberant Annemarie.

The cart started moving. The three girls on the narrow backseat clung to each other in order not to fall. The cart squeaked at every bend in the road. Annemarie would like to have held the arm of the stout coachman despite the heat. She rested perilously on the extreme edge. Her corpulent neighbor took almost the whole seat for himself.

Wagons and more wagons, all Berlin was on wheels. Father was right. Jests flew to and fro. The stately hunting cart with its blossoming occupants was a frequent target of Berlin wit.

Annemarie replied boldly. She was quick-witted and understood how to take a joke. Margot recoiled fearfully. Marianne giggled and laughed, Vera likewise, without understanding a word. They did not pay attention to where they were headed. But Margot, who was the most reliable, did not recognize the neighborhood.

"You, Annemie, ask the coachman if we get there soon." She tugged at her seated friend's rosebud dress.

"How far is it, Mr. Coachman?"

"We're almost there."

Worried, Annemarie looked around. "Is this the center of Berlin? We want to go to Alexanderplatz," she said, becoming more uncertain.

"Nope, this is Wedding," was the agreeable response.

"Oh, good heavens!" The teenagers looked at each other and broke into loud laughter.

"Kids, there is nothing to laugh about. How do we get to Alexanderplatz?" cried Margot, abruptly falling from a laughing into a tearful mood.

"In this cart." Annemarie was still carefree. "Mr. Coachman will get us there." The girl's blue eyes shone lovingly on the wagon's owner.

"Not any more," said the coachman. "My horse and me, we're through for the day. We're roasting to a crisp in this heat. We're heading back to the stable."

"But it's painted on your cart: Alexanderplatz. I read it clearly when I got on. How can you take us to Wedding?" piped up Marianne.

"Yes, and you relieved us of two marks for the trip." Even the shy Margot became courageous, since her modest pocket money was involved.

"Look, missy! Can't you read? Wedding-Alexanderplatz-Zoo is what's written. We always make a round trip, my Liese and I. Now we have arrived. Get out, if you please." The man was annoyed by the heat and the unjust accusation.

"Oh, Mr. Coachman," begged Annemarie with all her kindness. "Don't be a frog. Take us to Alexanderplatz. We will bring you a large piece of birthday cake from our friend's party. "

No luck.

"Nope, you can't ask that of me. My Liese wouldn't abide it."

"Liese looks so gentle." Annemarie's gaze caressed the flea-bitten nag, to no avail. The four girls had to bid farewell to Liese and her owner.

There they stood in the middle of sun drenched Wedding Place, in a completely different area of Berlin from where they wanted to be. The heat weighed like a heavy board on their heads.

"We did that up right. Three-horned camels, that's what we are," said Annemarie, falling into meditation.

"This animal is not in my zoology book," said Margot conscientiously.

"The coffee is cold. Certainly, they are eating the birthday cake now," wailed Marianne.

"I can skip the hot coffee. We need to get another wagon to Alexanderplatz," replied Annemarie.

"What? Again spend so much money?" said horrified Margot. "Can't we run?"

"Then we'll get there this evening. Margot, you're a stingy old thing."

"Besides, we can get heatstroke," added Annemarie firmly.

"There is a car to Alexanderplatz, an automobile. We will get there fast in it." Marianne pointed to a giant gray box rattling in a cloud of dust.

"Look what's written on it: *Berlin Refuse Company*. Pooh." Margot wrinkled her nose.

"Doesn't matter, we must get there quickly, before the cake is eaten," said Marianne, upset.

"Always forward. More people are getting in. The smell of manure is healthy," said the doctor's daughter.

Getting in was not so easy. The high back panel of the gray box had to be folded down, a ladder attached. In the scented interior the young ladies balanced themselves in their scented clothes. The panel was closed behind them.

"Pew, devil take it, this is air?" In the heat the smell was twice as vile. "Where is our vibrant perfume bottle? Come, Marianne, you have to put yourself between us, otherwise we will faint." They reached toward their fragrantly violet-perfumed girlfriend.

The uninviting garbage truck had neither benches nor chairs. Passengers were standing, packed like sardines. In every corner they fell over each other, screaming. They didn't want to hold on to the dirty truck.

"Like Noah's Ark," said Annemarie, whose humor never failed.

"Hopefully we won't see the flood," said Vera, peering up at the sky.

Oops, what was happening? A short while ago the sky was blue. The white haze had thickened into heavy, threatening clouds. Weak and thin, a last sunbeam emerged.

Had Mother's bones been right?

"We'll be there before the cloudburst. Our excellent manure wagon is racing like the devil and his grandmother." Annemarie's cheer recklessly retained the upper hand.

But the approaching storm was moving faster than the Berlin Refuse Company. A gust of wind, a cloud of dust that prevented anyone from opening her eyes: that was the beginning. The first drops were heavy and slow. And now a dazzling zigzag, as the air waves boiled. Immediately after came a crash, deafening, shocking, and horrifying. Margot, afraid of storms, cried out in terror, and the others clung anxiously to each other.

As if the mouth of hell had opened its corrupting gorge, the air was lit with sulfur-yellow fire. Flash on flash, roaring, crashing, bursting. The patter of rain accompanied the lashing thunder storm. Relentless rain turned delicate sun dresses soggy in the open carriage. Like a cold shower bath, the rain flowed over the exposed passengers.

"It feels good." One passenger removed his hat and let the rain run off him. "It does feel good," said another, drawing in a deep breath.

Opinion was divided. The four teenagers, almost swimming, gazed in horror at their drenched condition.

O God, the rosebud dress! Dripping and unsightly as a mop, it stuck to its hunched owner, and would be of no use in a dance lesson. Vera tried to wash off tea spots with rainwater. Excited Marianne forgot the cake. Margot saw nothing. She held her fear-filled eyes tightly closed.

Finally the girls arrived.

A little black brook rippled from their hair and clothes into the clean apartment on Ulrichstraße.

They were eagerly awaited.

"That's what happens when you decide to appear so late. If you had been on time, you would have avoided the bad weather," reproached the birthday girl.

"We took a little tour after we got to Wedding."

"Heavens, you look like four scarecrows. You smell like a dung heap!" Ilse held her nose.

"We were transported by the Berlin Refuse Company." The cheerful Annemarie was quite meek. The spoiled dress and uncomfortable wetness were to blame.

"Children, you can not stand next to my upholstery and carpets. Come into the bathroom. We'll make you somewhat human again." Mrs. Ulrich laughed with Marlene and Ilse at the four sad figures.

"Best would be to put the whole group together with their clothes into the bathtub," suggested Marlene, who was not exactly enchanted with the fragrant birthday greeting.

"Yes, a bath for the whole family." The four girls were uncomfortable in their own skin.

Marianne wanted a piece of birthday cake. But she had to accept the majority decision: first came cleanliness.

Laughing and giggling sounded from the bathroom. Marlene's mother had to knock several times so that the neighbors would not complain. It took a long while before the four pure, washed virgins appeared in strange disguises. The coffee table had turned into a dinner table, so late was the hour. But the girls got birthday cake.

"We wanted dearly to celebrate Marlene's birthday on the water. Basically, that's what we did." Annemarie, in a housecoat of Marlene's mother that came to her feet, was not at a loss for words.

The four dung beetles, as Ilse had baptized them, retained a long memory of their outing with the Berlin Refuse Company in their tainted clothes.

Chapter 8.
At Work on the Harvest

"Girl, you've grown into a young lady in the four years since I last saw you, a proper young lady. But your merry blue eyes are still the same." With work-roughened fists Uncle Henry grabbed his pretty niece by both ears.

"I hope you've not become a Berlin ornamental doll," amiably remarked Cousin Peter, who was enthroned on the box of the carriage and held the reins.

"Nah, high school girls are not ornamental dolls," Annemarie said with a clear conscience.

She and her luggage were loaded. Peter clucked and the horses pulled.

"Peter, let me have the reins." Annemarie climbed on the box beside him.

"You can't; you need to learn. Latin is not the main subject in life." Peter did not think much of book learning. He wanted to run a farm like his father and sought practical knowledge. In addition, the two cousins, Peter and Herbert, harbored the secret fear that their attractive cousin had become an ornament or a bluestocking. She was like all the Berlin girls, especially high school girls.

"Give me the reins; it's easy!" Energetically Annemarie took the reins from her cousin, who was not much older. She did well. On the straight avenue of poplars that led to Arnsdorf Farm from the train, the carriage rolled by itself. The horses knew the way. They did not particularly care who held the reins. The young charioteer had time to admire the luminous poppies that nodded from golden straws.

"It costs in Berlin two marks for a puny bouquet. Can I pluck one for Aunt Kate?" The big city child found it difficult to breeze past the tempting flowers.

"We have enough of those weeds at home, girl. Forward! "

Fields, meadows, forests and a clear blue sky were so bright that Anne Marie's blue eyes shone back. Far from the big city was this child's heart.

"Should we drive through the village, Annemie?" Peter saw something suspicious in Annemarie's small fists.

"Nah, absolutely not! In the village they'll make fun of me."

But she wanted to show off her new skills to the residents who greeted the lords of the manor in brightly knitted peasant clothes.

In the village pond waded barefoot children. The teenage girl would have liked to take off her shoes and stockings.

At first everything went perfectly. If only the Dear God had created no cows, who had the audacity, returning from pasture, to plant themselves in the middle of the village street. With their enormous staring eyes they looked contemptuously at the city lady driving the coach.

"Grasp the reins firmly. Straight ahead," commanded Peter.

What? We should roll right through the herd of cows? Nah, no one could ask her to do that. The cows did not know how easily they could puncture your legs with their horns.

The horses felt the uncertainty of the new coachman. They were restless, began to balk and shy away from the herd of cows.

The cows bellowed in shock. Louder still roared Doctor's Nesthäkchen: "Uncle Henry the cows will eat our horses!" With expertise Peter grasped the reins and brought the horses to a halt.

"You silly dame: how can you be afraid of cows?" The gallant cousin looked at Annemarie more contemptuously than the cows had.

Behind them rang out Uncle Henry's booming laughter. "You're a pip of a girl to prostrate yourself in front of a herd of cows." The pastor in his black velvet cap in the open window of the parish house chortled, his head bobbing up and down.

The townsfolk in the village square laughed, put their heads together, and whispered about the new girl. The chickens clucked and laughed. The golden cross on the steeple sparkled and laughed in the fading light. And the evening sun, grinning with her wide, beaming face, doused Annemarie with purple-red.

Doctor's Nesthäkchen had made her entry into Arnsdorf.

When Aunt Kate, Mother's sister, heartily joined arms with her young guest, Annemarie could see that she was no longer shorter than her aunt, and quickly forgot her misadventures. Cousin Elli, the dear girl, stretched out her arms to Annemarie in welcome. Herbert, the twenty year old cousin who Annemarie had always teased, stood nearby.

"My boy, you've now got a mustache!" said Annemarie.

"Yours is still growing, Annemie, if you're a student." He ribbed her about her education.

Old August, who was on the farm with Uncle Henry's father, extended his calloused hand. Mina still rattled around with colorful striped stockings in her wooden clogs. Pluto was there, the massive Newfoundland dog, who once had profound respect for Nesthäkchen; and Waldmann, Uncle's dachshund, waddling and bowlegged, whose wisdom was reported to be miraculous. Everything was familiar, yet new again and transformed.

The dinner table on the veranda, braided with climbing roses, filled the city child with bright enthusiasm.

"Yuck, sour milk! This stuff became quite unfashionable in Berlin during the war. And ham! I know it only from fairy tales. Can you eat so many slices? Can you keep within your bread ration? "Annemarie exuded joy with her questions.

"You do not look like a starved Berliner, lass." Uncle Henry pinched her rosy cheeks.

"Because you always sent such fine food packages for us and Grandma," responded Annemarie laughing.

"It will be eaten quickly, once we are Polish," Peter said while chewing.

"What? Here in Upper Silesia you will become Polish? I am very fond of the Poles. The mother of my best friend Vera was Polish. Vera's father was killed in the Carpathian battle.[29] Vera

---

[29] On May 3, 1915, during a 10-day-long stretch of fighting in the Carpathian Mountains on the Galician front in Austria-Hungary, a combined Austro-German force succeeded in defeating the Russian army.

has not seen her brother for years; he lives with Polish relatives." Anne Marie's motor mouth slobbered as she prattled on. She did not notice how her uncle angrily arched his blond eyebrows into a small bristling forest. Reproachfully Aunt Kate gestured at Peter, who continued to chew.

Elli and Herbert made embarrassed faces and tried to avoid talking about the imminent Polish occupation of this stretch of land on the Polish frontier. Uncle Henry was enraged that German land should fall into Polish hands.[30]

Annemarie in her happy innocence did not notice the ominous pause.

"I almost didn't come," she chattered cheerfully. "The day before yesterday I did not know whether the railway men would go on strike. Margot Thielen, my best friend, was happy that I would have to stay home. Now I'm sitting here with oxen and geese."

---

[30] In 1742, most of Silesia was seized by King Frederick the Great of Prussia in the War of the Austrian Succession, becoming the Prussian Province of Silesia. Silesia became part of the German Empire when it was proclaimed in 1871. After World War I, Upper Silesia was contested by Germany and the newly independent Second Polish Republic. Poland occupied and was ceded some Silesian territory, 1919-1922, in the aftermath of World War I, the Polish Czechoslovak War of 1919, and the Treaty of Versailles.

"The society in which you find yourself is flattered." The cloud over Uncle Henry's forehead disappeared, confronted with Annemarie's uninhibited merriment.

"We want you to get fed, my girl. You are undernourished in the big city." Aunt Kate reveled in the bright joy of her lively niece.

"I did not come for the food, Aunt Kate," assured Anne Marie. "I'm supposed to help with the harvest."

"Ha ha ha," the cousins laughed in unison.

"You come from Berlin. You can translate Virgil and Cicero, but you can't distinguish barley from wheat, and you want to help with the harvest? That's rich!"

"Enough, Herbert." Twenty year old gentlemen had not impressed the teenage girl for a long time. "Wait and see who helps more, you or me."

"It does not take much to outdo Herbert," said Elli, amused at the dispute. Her elder brother, now at home on vacation, was exceptionally slothful and showed little interest in agriculture; that's why he wanted to study engineering, not take over the farm.

"Watch out for cows if you wish to help with the harvest, Annemie." Peter mischievously winked his left eye. "They sometimes go wild and charge."

Annemarie pushed and poked her impudent cousin covertly under the table, as though he were Klaus.

The glass of milk that Aunt Kate filled for the second time flew into the air.

Was Aunt Kate angry? She rebuked with a smile: "I'm glad we have an oilcloth and no tableware."

"Hanne would scold differently if I spilled the beautiful milk that we are lucky to get every other day." Annemie looked regretfully at the white lake. Oh, if she could send a letter home about it!

"Annemarie must report for harvest work," announced Uncle Heinrich, large clouds of smoke billowing from his pipe. "Tomorrow morning at four on the field, understand?"

"Up at four?" Shocked blue eyes stared at Uncle Henry. "There's no point going to bed."

"You think that here we bring the gracious lady her chocolate at nine o'clock in bed?" interjected Peter.

"Nope, that's not the case in Berlin. I must be at school by eight. Anyway, I recently got up at four thirty to go on a foraging trip," responded the teenage girl.

"Let the child alone. She is to rest here." Aunt Kate took the part of her niece. "Sleep as long as you wish, Annemie. If you want to help me in the garden, with the poultry, or in the dairy, I will be happy."

"Help with housework if you want to show us that you have not become a bluestocking." This Peter was almost more disgusting than Klaus.

"I could use a nanny for my toddler," Elli added to the banter. She was a war bride. Her husband was recently assigned to Kiel to serve as a magistrate. She could find, due to the housing shortage that prevailed everywhere, no suitable apartment. Therefore, Elli and her boy were living with her parents.

"Oh, yeah, I like that best; I know how I do it. Everyone will have my help. In the morning I will work at the harvest. Then I'll give Aunt Kate a hand, and in the afternoon comes my reward: your boy."

"I shall be praying that you do not let me down. Workers are scarce, and the annoyance with the Poles does not recede." Uncle made as serious a face as possible. "Whoever wants to eat should work."

"So tomorrow morning at four clock!" Annemarie yawned furtively. She was tired from her trip. "Have you an alarm clock?"

"The cock wakes us. Goodnight, Annemie."

Doctor's Nesthäkchen stood in her charming room with its gabled window and view across the yard, the barn, and the meadow, bathed in the dim light of the moon. In long breaths she inhaled the spicy hay-scented air that mixed with the night wind. Somewhere a calf bleated. Hark! The nightingale sang, tender and sweet. For a long time the city kid stood, listening to the breath of nature. God's peace was here!

When Uncle Henry rode out the next morning, soon after four o'clock, onto the fields, he cast up a sly glance at the windows of the gabled room. The green shutters were firmly closed.

Two hours later, Aunt Kate began her tour of the poultry farm, the calf nursery and the orchard. She peered up at her niece's room. It was obvious that the girl was tired after her long journey.

The toddler appeared at half past seven, freshly washed and rested. But his new aunt, who wanted to play with him, was not in attendance.

Peter, who had risen at the crack of dawn, hungrily joined his father for second breakfast, while Herbert was drinking his coffee.

"Has our dear cousin crawled out of bed?"

"She sleeps like a rat. She's lazier than I am."

"We want to bring her back from dreamland to reality." Green apples had been knocked down by the wind. Peter gathered them up and pelted the green shutters of the gabled room.

Inside Annemie sprang up frightened. "Heavens, they're shooting." That was certainly a bomb! The shutters slid and the glass shattered.

Was there Revolution again? Spartacist unrest?[31]

Annemarie was a spirited girl. With both legs she jumped out of bed to see what was going on.

---

[31] The Spartacist uprising, also known as the January uprising, was a general strike (and the armed battles accompanying it) in Germany from 4 to 15 January 1919. Germany was in the middle of a post-war revolution, and the two paths forward were social democracy or a council/soviet republic similar to the one which had been established by the Bolshevik Party in Russia. The uprising was primarily a power struggle between the moderate Social Democratic Party of Germany led by Friedrich Ebert, and the more radical communists of the Communist Party of Germany, led by Karl Liebknecht and Rosa Luxemburg, who had previously founded and led the Spartacist League. This power struggle was the result of the abdication of Kaiser Wilhelm II and the resignation of Chancellor Max von Baden, who had passed power onto Ebert as the leader of the largest party in the German parliament. Similar uprisings occurred and were suppressed in Bremen, the Ruhr, Rhineland, Saxony, Hamburg, Thuringia and Bavaria, and another round of even bloodier street battles occurred in Berlin in March, which led to popular disillusionment with the Weimar Government.

Having overslept, she looked around her foreign environment.

Jeez, she was not in Berlin in her own room. She was on Arnsdorf Farm. Were the Poles, the targets of last night's wrath, shooting at the farm? Annemarie ventured a few steps toward the window.

She rebounded with a horrified cry.

The shutters were blown open, "a bomb, a bomb." Annemarie held her bleeding nose against the shutter which the bomb had grazed.

Peter laughed loudly.

A disheveled blonde with anxiously staring blue eyes and a bloody nose stood at the gabled window. "Peter, Peterchen, shoot them. The Poles are bombing the house." Two laughing boys drowned out further cries for help from the teenage girl. The cousins were clasping their stomachs with mirth.

"Don't let the Poles kill you, Annemie." That cry didn't sound dangerous. Annemarie took a closer look at the terrible bullet that had wounded her nose: a harmless grass-green apple.

"Darn brat!" In an instant Annemarie realized that her cousins had got the best of her. Just wait! Gripping the water jug, she let its cold contents spill on the revelers below. Take that!

"Little toad!" The two no longer laughed. They crept away like drowned rats. Now it was Annemarie's turn to laugh: "In the event that the Poles burned the farm, I wanted to put out the fire immediately."

The sun shone hot on the fields, when a charming peasant girl appeared in a black flowered dress and rose-red kerchief at the breakfast table. Four o'clock was long gone. Annemarie did not suspect that it was almost ten. Fatigued from yesterday's travel, she had forgotten to wind her watch.

Herbert was reading a book in a deck chair under the walnut tree. He was dry again. "Blessed mealtime, Annemie," he greeted her. "Do you want more coffee? We'll have lunch soon."

"What time is it?"

"Quarter to twelve. A pity that the Polish bomb woke you from your slumber; you would have awakened only when you were ready to leave for Berlin."

"You would have had to give up your morning shower." Annemarie drank her milk, and ate golden yellow butter and honey on a slice of country bread. She liked dining with her cousins.

As a city girl, she was ashamed that she had slept so late in the day. Though Herbert was joking about the time, it wasn't early. Midday haze was obscuring the clarity of the midsummer morning.

Aunt Kate's work was not easy. Annemarie peeked in the warm cowshed. The cows grumbled, full and satisfied, swatting buzzing flies with their tails; they stared in astonishment at the peasant girl. The stable air was anything but refreshing. "It's funny that people always say cow stall air is healthy," thought Annemarie sniffing. "I think it smells like the Berlin Refuse Company."

Aunt Kate was not in the barn. The young city dweller did not dare venture far inside. A cow was unpredictable. It might knock Annemarie's legs from under her and no one would notice. Hopefully she need not be here to help during milking, which she would never survive.

Aunt Kate was not next door in the calf nursery, either. Annemarie found the nursery more agreeable. The clumsy, soft, delicate creatures jumped and played. The courtiers all seemed to be in the field at harvest time. Not a soul was present. Old August, with his straight hanging gray hair, was in the sheep stall.

Annemarie was glad to see a human being.

"Good morning, August, have you seen my aunt some-where?"

"No, no, no," said August in his fine Silesian dialect. "She's in the fruit garden selecting the bears."

"You have bears on the farm?" asked Annemarie uncomfortably.

"Currants—they're ripe."[32]

Annemarie bit her lip to keep from laughing out loud. Good that her cousins had not heard.

"Oh, I must be there, I like to eat currants for my health," said August. Annemarie was still laughing at the old man and his bears.

"Go through the gate and you'll see your aunt." August pointed Annemarie in the general direction.

Annemarie walked where August had pointed. She did not see her aunt and ended up in the orchard on the pasture. Bleating goats jumped toward her.

In the midst of the troubled meh meh meh that did not fit the exuberant leaps, a child's voice cried out.

"Bübchen," shouted Annemarie, approaching the toddler.

---

[32] Else Ury is playing with the words Bären (bears) and Beeren (berries).

At the forest edge, Elli sat busy with needlework. Bübchen with his short, thick legs was clumsily trying to imitate the articulated jumps of the quadrupeds. Elli held her sides with laughter. The little fellow shouted because his mother laughed. As bright as a bell, the schoolgirl's laughter mixed with the voices of the other two.

"Well, Annemie, you actually made it out of bed?" said her cousin happily. "Can I use a nanny who does not need to get up until ten o'clock?"

"Oh, Elli, is it really so late?"

"Were you with Father this morning in the field? Are you already home?" Elli made a hypocritical face.

"Of course, I have harvested some wheat." Annemarie elaborated on the joke.

"Pity we are now harvesting rye," laughed Elli. "If you had come sooner, you could have helped Mother making juice."

"I'll do it in your place," promised Anne Marie. "I must let Aunt Kate know that I am finally awake."

The jubilant Bübchen rolled around a couple of times on the green velvet carpet. Annemarie trotted off to the industrial farm kitchen after a respectful bow to the pasture. So many clumsy jumping goat legs do not exactly inspire confidence.

A huge stove occupied the center of the basement kitchen. Aunt Kate stood with flushed face, no less red than the red juice that she heated in a copper kettle. Mademoiselle was engaged in pressing the "bears."

"Morning, Aunt Kate, can I help?"

"Of course, my girl, are you well rested?"

"Oh, Aunt Kate, tomorrow I'll prove that my stopped watch was to blame for my getting up late."

At Aunt Kate's direction, Annemarie spread cheesecloth over a wide, low wooden barrel.

"Hold tight, Annemie, hold firmly." Aunt Kate and Mademoiselle took ladles and began to pour the purple berry juice through the cloth.

The cloth was hot. It was heavy and sticky. Annemarie's arms started to weaken. The giant boiler was over half full. More and more, more and more, endlessly, without pause, the hot red juice ran through the spread out cloth.

Annemarie found herself thinking that translating Virgil was far from the worst task. Your thoughts might become lame, but not your arms.

Through the open kitchen window buzzed a formidable black Bumblebee. With a loud, deep grumbling it circled the new cook. She had never seen such a huge bee. Was it attracted by the sweet red juice?

The bee, a monster, a black monster, flew in narrowing circles around Annemarie's blond head. Annemarie left the juice to fend for itself and ran her hand against her rosy cheek, which the black behemoth had treacherously undertaken to attack.

Plop! Cloth, juice, berries and seeds followed each other into the barrel.

"Girl, you ought to have held on firmly. Now all our work is for nothing." Aunt Kate suppressed with difficulty her displeasure.

"Do not scold, Aunt Kate. That black beast was determined to sting me." Actually, Annemarie was glad that she got away in this manner from the tiring work. It was too late to start from the beginning.

The village clock chimed noon. Lunchtime in Arnsdorf occurred punctually at twelve o'clock.

In the cool room with the heavy tankards lining the darkly paneled wooden wall ledge, the family members reassembled.

Father and son brought home fierce hunger from the field.

"Good morning, Annemie. So, did the nocturnal raid of the Poles go well?" Peter inquired with special friendliness.

Before Annemarie could parry the blow with repartee, Uncle Henry angrily struck his fist on the table so energetically that the full soup terrine overflowed onto the oilcloth.

"At mealtimes I want peace. All morning I have to cope with Polish workers who act like they own this farm. They are all disobedient. I have hardly eaten my first spoonful of soup, and back to the Poles we go." Anne Marie never thought that nice Uncle Henry could get so angry!

"It was a joke, Uncle Henry. Peter wanted to tease me." She took the part of her cousin, who did not deserve her intervention.

Uncle Henry's bright blue eyes were again friendly to the young visitor. He realized that he had been carried away by unpleasant gossip in the village about the advance of Polish troops.

"Yes, you see, Little One, if you leave me in the lurch with the harvest, I am dependent on the Poles," he relented.

"I can begin the harvest work this afternoon," suggested Annemarie. "I am sure that I will not oversleep."

"Who knows?" commented Herbert, expressing his concern. "Back in the garden between the pines is the hammock. You can sleep there until evening."

"I won't fight with you over it," responded Annemarie with a laugh.

At three o'clock on the dot, Doctor's Nesthäkchen waited, as arranged, at the farm gate, to meet her uncle after his nap. Peter and Waldmann were there.

"You need to cover your head, lass, the sun is quite bright," Uncle Henry pointed out.

"A parasol instead of a scythe: that would be something new for the harvest." It would have been nicer if Peter had not come. At the end she disgraced herself in front of him.

"I'd like a tan. We six girlfriends have made a bet on who will be crispiest after the holidays; the ones at the lake, probably. I think that Margot Thielen, who had to stay at home, is every day rubbing her face with salt water and then sitting on the balcony in the sun. She doesn't want to be left out."

A cart, dazzling white in the bright midday sun, ran through the insect filled meadow. Pink carnations, bluebells, bright blue and white daisies, and golden dandelions bloomed and glowed in the sunshine. The city child could not bring herself to pass by them. She began here and there to pick and arrange the flowers for a bouquet.

"You call that harvest work? The hay-making is over," ribbed her cousin.

"Annemie, if we continue to crawl at this snail's pace," said Uncle Henry, "we'll be in this same spot tomorrow morning." Annemie stuck the colorful bouquet in her bodice and rushed after the two men.

At the lush foal paddock, a small brook rippled over the pasture. A herd of cows lay lazily ruminating. Their bells rang out a confused melody. Not far from the road stood a magnificent mottled animal that raised its head against the bright sky and loudly, joyfully roared.

Doctor's Nesthäkchen winced. "Is that a bull?"

"Yes, but he does nothing if you don't provoke him. Oh God, you're wearing red cloth, Annemie. You'll set him wild." Peter grinned with delight at his new joke.

Annemarie, in her excitement, saw only the bull. She tore off the red cloth kerchief, concealed it under her green apron, and jumped over the babbling brook to the meadow on the other side to escape the fury of the bull. She accomplished this feat in a second.

Whoops! Her legs were not long enough, and she splashed into the water with a belly flop. Doctor's Youngest lay in the creek, while the water cooled her.

On the bank of the creek, trimmed with forget-me-nots, the two gentlemen laughed and laughed.

"Annemie, the bull is a cow! You've busted your buns on account of a cow!" Peter hooted with delight.

"How did I know? You monkey's tail! Help me out of this water. Don't stand there bleating." Annemarie was upset and she knew who was to blame.

A dripping water sprite emerged from the silvery wetness with pitiful eyes, which were as blue as the forget-me-nots on the bank.

"Stand in the sun, Annemie. When we come back to pick you up, you'll be dry."

One should not mock the afflicted.

"Not there; about face, girl; you need to put on dry clothes quickly, so you don't catch cold," commanded Uncle Henry.

"What? I can't do the harvest work?" Annemarie was boundlessly disappointed.

"The scarecrow has harvested enough rye." Klaus was not nearly as ungallant as Peter.

Annemarie had to go back to the house.

"Shall I escort you and protect you, like a knight in shining armor, from bulls and similar beasts you might encounter?" the youth asked with a deep bow.

Doctor's Nesthäkchen did not deign to answer. With a quick step, her head turned away, she glanced uneasily at the comfortable ruminant quadrupeds.

A bull was among them.

Chapter 9.
The Unforeseen

It was the third week of Annemarie's stay at Arnsdorf Farm. She had learned not to see an angry bull in every harmless cow. She was saddled with fieldwork and had cut her little finger with a sharp scythe. Despite a burning July sun, Annemarie diligently helped with separating and binding the sheaves. She looked in need of relaxation, like other "starved city dwellers," said Peter, but she had accomplished a feat that seemed harder than the hardest mathematical calculation.

"Girl, you have done good work," Uncle Henry remarked appreciatively. "How can I go about hiring you? Would you like a salary plus room and board?"

"Father needs me to be his assistant. My brothers do not want to study medicine. I've promised father; otherwise, Uncle Henry, I would consider your offer." Annemarie took the matter seriously.

Filled with good will, Annemarie had helped Aunt Kate with cooking, as well as in the vegetable and fruit garden. The high spirited girl had won her over so completely that Auntie was loath to see her go. "I don't want to give you back; you've got to stay with me, my darling, if Elli and Bübchen move to Kiel and leave me forever," she often said.

"You can marry me," Peter suggested.

"What a stupid idea. Nope, such a smart aleck I do not want for a husband." Annemarie declined peremptorily.

"What's the matter with me?" teased Herbert.

"You would be ideal, right? A sloth is worse than a rascal." Despite their daily verbal battles and baiting, the cousins understood each other well.

Annemarie was loved most of all by Bübchen, even more than by Waldmann, who ran after her everywhere. Bübchen wanted to be fed only by Annemarie, who had to give him his bottle, wash him and put him to bed. If Bübchen saw Annemarie, "Mie," as he called her, from a distance, he would not allow his mother to hold him. "What will happen when my nanny goes back to high school in Berlin?" wailed Elli.

"Until then, we have an awfully long time," consoled Annemarie. For the time being, there were still weeks full of golden sun and unbound freedom for Doctor's Nesthäkchen.

Every morning before the mirror while combing her hair— there was no other time to stand at the mirror in Arnsdorf-- Annemarie noted triumphantly that she was burned brown. If the browning went on a few more weeks, she would be able to compete with Marlene and Ilse for the chocolate kiss prize.

Figure 5. Despite a burning July sun, Annemarie diligently helped with separating and binding the sheaves.

It was notable that the Polish agricultural workers, usually grumpy and grudging, liked Annemarie.

"Do not get too close to them; stay out of their way, child. They're up to no good," warned Aunt Kate.

But Annemarie was used to greeting everyone in a friendly way. Her radiant blue eyes had enchanted the Polish laborers. Her red rose scarf, decorated with colorful farm flowers, attracted the eyes of the Polish women. When the young city dweller was bailing hay one morning, a Polish woman with sparkling black eyes approached her.

"Ah, beautiful cloth, beautiful cloth," the woman said admiringly, passing a caressing hand over the bright cloth.

Was the Polish woman trying to rob her of the cloth? Annemarie took one furtive look around. The other workers were quite far away from them. Besides, they were almost exclusively Poles and would hardly stand for such a thing. On a whim Annemarie tore off the cloth and handed it to the surprised woman.

"Do you want to have the beautiful cloth? Here you go; I'll give it to you."

The Polish woman was beside herself with joy. "Ah, gutte Frräulein beautiful Frräulein." She could not bestow enough grateful kisses on Annemarie's hand. From that day on Annemarie was the declared favorite of the Polish working class.

"A diminutive satanic witch," chuckled Uncle Henry. "With the Poles she is a good friend."

The friendship proved to be enlightening.

One July evening, the lime trees smelled sweet and heavy. Annemarie stood at her gabled window and loosened her thick blond hair for the night. The air was delicious. The young girl could not decide whether to lock the shutters.

A dark shadow appeared on the moonlit white wall of the house.

»Fräulein, gutte Frräulein, beautiful Frräulein, Maruschka wants sprrechen to gutte Frräulein," whispered a voice carried up by the night wind.

"What do you want?" Annemarie asked aloud. She had no fear, although she was not quite comfortable.

"Ah sprrechen not loud, sprrechen quietly, very quietly. Maruschka wants to say something to gutte Frräulein, who has given poor Polish woman beautiful rred cloth. If gutte Frräulein wants to travel home to Maminka, can not travel after tomorrow."

"Why, Maruschka, will there be a railway strike?" Annemarie dampened her bright voice. She felt that the grateful Polish lady meant well.

"Poles coming. They take farm, town, railroad. Gutte Frräulein can not travel home to Maminka after tomorrow."

"I thank you, Maruschka. But the situation isn't that bad." With the carelessness of youth Annemarie shoved aside any possibility of an early interruption of her wonderful stay in Arnsdorf. Nonsense, it was drivel that the border area here would be occupied by advancing Polish soldiers! That was certainly one of the most popular rumors, carefree Nesthäkchen thought as she fell asleep.

When Annemarie came down to breakfast the next morning, she was surprised that the master of the house, who had taken his morning ride, was there to meet her.

"Uncle Henry, you're here? Fine! We can go together to the field after we finish eating," she cried vividly.

"You will not be able to go to the field, child." Uncle Henry had deep wrinkles between his blond eyebrows.

"Why not?" Anne Marie's eyes were round and amazed. They wandered from scowling Uncle Henry to Aunt Kate. Oops? Was Aunt Kate crying?

"Annemie, we have been officially informed that strong Polish forces are advancing on Arnsdorf. They will occupy our property and cut us off entirely from our German fatherland." Gentle Aunt Kate cried, her tears hot with indignation.

"Oh, Aunt Kate, as you have said yourself, no one should believe these silly rumors," consoled Annemarie.

The night warning of Maruschka: had Aunt Kate heard the rumor, too?

"This time it's serious. It is reported officially," interjected Uncle Henry.[33] "Child, under the forthcoming precarious condi-

---

[33] The Silesian Uprisings were a series of three armed uprisings of the Poles and Polish Silesians of Upper Silesia, from 1919 to 1921, against German rule; the resistance hoped to break away from Germany in order to join the Second Polish Republic, which had been established in the wake of World War I. On 15 August 1919, German border guards massacred ten Silesian civilians in a labor dispute at the Mysłowice mine. The massacre sparked protests from the Silesian Polish miners, including a general strike of about 140,000 workers, and caused the First Silesian Uprising against German control of Upper Silesia, which Else Ury alludes to here. The miners demanded the local government and police become ethnically mixed to include both Germans and Poles. About 21,000 Germans soldiers of the Weimar Republic's Provisional National Army, with about 40,000 troops held in reserve, quickly put down the uprising. The army's reaction was harsh; and about 2,500 Poles were either hanged or executed by firing squad for their parts in the violence. Some 9,000 ethnic Poles sought refuge in the Second Polish Republic, taking along their family members. The conflict came

tions we can not bear the responsibility to your parents. We do not know how long the trains will continue to run. As hard as it is for us, Annemarie, Aunt Kate and I believe that you should immediately pack your things. We will telegraph your parents."

"What? You want to kick me out?" interrupted the teen-age girl with quivering lips? Uncle Henry and Aunt Kate, who never wanted to give her up? They wanted her out today? Annemarie could not believe her ears.

"Annemiechen, darling, do you know how hard it was for us to decide to take this step?" Aunt Kate drew the frozen girl tenderly toward her. "But it has to be. We can no longer vouch for your safety here. We would love to send Elli and her boy with you. But they will certainly never leave us."

"Neither will I. I want to remain with you, Aunt Kate. I am not a bit frightened of the Poles. Don't throw me out, please, please."

To refuse the begging blue eyes was a hard piece of work.

But Uncle Henry shook his head. "You could be cut off for months from your parents. We can not risk it. You must pack your bags immediately. We will take you to the station. You can catch the eleven o'clock train to Breslau. Herbert will accompa-

---

to an end when Allied forces were brought in to restore order, and the refugees were allowed to return later that year.

ny you to Breslau. In Breslau you can change to the train for Berlin. Sorry, kid, but it's not the worst or most painful sacrifice that the Poles demand of us." Uncle Henry stomped out to the porch.

For the first time since her Arnsdorf stay began, breakfast did not zip by. Annemarie choked on the tasty country bread and golden honey that she otherwise enjoyed immensely. She tried to draw out the meal.

It did not help. Her suitcase was brought up. Elli helped Annemarie pack, while Aunt Kate prepared a gift food package for her parents and a snack for the journey.

As in a dream, everything seemed to Annemarie unreal, as if she were not personally experiencing it. There was the coachman August, who loaded her suitcases on the cart. Annemarie clung to the arms of Aunt Kate; she did not want to let go. Bübchens voice called out, "Take me, Mie, Mie, take me." Waldmann's golden brown dachshund tail waved in the blue air.

She passed meadows, cows, fields, waving sheaves that she had tied by hand, and the red church of Arnsdorf. Farewell!

Black smoke belched from the roaring steam locomotive. People bustled. Through a veil of tears Annemarie watched Uncle Henry's broad figure and Peter's lean one on the platform grow smaller and smaller. The train rounded a curve and Arnsdorf disappeared.

Annemarie pulled out her handkerchief and wept bitterly.

Herbert did not quite know what to do with the howling girl. Annemarie's impetuous outbreak of pain was embarrassing. The train was crowded. Everyone wanted to get out before the Poles arrived.

At Breslau, Herbert left his cousin to her fate.

"Good bye, Annemarie, when we have kicked out the Poles, you can come back," he cried consolingly, running along beside the moving train.

Annemie shook her head sadly. When would that be? It seemed to her as if her departing cousin represented the last drop of the golden days of summer in the country.

The best consolation for farewell pain was the food basket. When Annemarie ate the first egg and the delicious ham sandwich, they became her painkillers. She had in the morning scattered the feed for the hens that had donated her egg. The ham came certainly from the ancestor of one of the rosy pigs that had so drolly burrowed, to Anne Marie's delight, in the sand. And the peaches she herself had picked from the trellis yesterday. Affectionately Annemarie stroked their velvet. They felt as soft as Bübchen's cheek.

The train rattled onward, putting an ever greater distance between Nesthäkchen and her happy vacation. How might it be in Arnsdorf when the Poles came? Her fellow travelers told of all sorts of Polish attacks, hardship and unbearable pressure in occupied territory. The young girl could not imagine quite so bad a situation. Maruschka had been so good to her. And Vera had Polish blood in her veins.

What would Margot say if Annemarie suddenly pounded the balcony wall? And Annemarie's parents! How happy they would be to have their Lotte again. Annemarie was sad but felt pleasure picturing the joy of her parents. The thought warmed her heart. She would see everyone again, if Uncle Henry had in his excitement remembered to telegraph. She was to arrive in Berlin at night.

She had enough money to afford a cab from the train station. Generous Uncle Henry had given her a hundred mark note that was carefully placed in her handbag. Spasmodically she held the bag in her hand and looked at every fellow traveler suspiciously, whether or not he entertained evil intentions toward her treasure.

Gradually her suspicion dwindled. She befriended the other passengers. This simple, friendly creature, a teenage girl, soon won everyone's heart.

The Riesengebirge with their blue gray mountainous ridges appeared at the window. Legnica with its old houses passed by, then forests, meadows, windmills--red and white headscarves between golden stalks.

Evening roses flourished in purple splendor under the western sky. The train pulled into the station concourse of Sagan.[34] It was not far to Berlin, three and a half hours. Annemarie could hardly wait.

The conductor entered her compartment. "Sagan, everyone off, the train goes no further."

Oops, what does that mean?

The conductor headed to the next compartment to repeat his announcement.

Confusion was everywhere. Two ladies snatched anxiously at their copious hand luggage. A gentleman cursed but did not stir from his place. He had paid his fare to Berlin and wished to be transported there. Another passenger urged him to exit. But why should he? Surely something was wrong with the locomotive; a second one would be brought out in due course.

This idea made sense to Annemarie. She grabbed her things. Ample luggage though it was, Aunt Kate had not ex-

---

[34] Sagan (now Żagań, western Poland) is a Silesian town 200 km SE of Berlin.

pected Annemarie to need a change of clothes between Breslau and Berlin, where she was expected to meet her parents at the station. Two egg boxes, one for Grandmother, one for the parents, a heavy backpack strapped to them. Then there was the basket which beeped softly, containing young chicks. Annemarie did not know how she should deal with her belongings.

At last she stood in a knot of people on the platform, illuminated by the evening sun. They besieged the man with the red cap, who shrugged his shoulders indifferently: "Railway strike proclaimed, no more trains."

"I have to get to Berlin," shouted an angry man.

"Hire an airship," cried some joker.

The travelers circled each other in indescribable agitation. Everyone hoped in vain that somewhere an opportunity to travel existed. The black, snarling iron behemoths stood pitilessly still. No wheel turned. The strike had rudely interrupted all traffic.

Annemarie was dazed. What now? Her parents would worry about her absence. Above all, she must send a telegram home. The teenage girl could sometimes be uncaring and inconsiderate. Not now. This was an hour that demanded wisdom.

The post office stood opposite. Annemarie put the back-pack, egg crates and chirping luggage into a storage space.

In front of the post office was a tense queue of people. All wanted to send telegrams. The first to enter came back out of the post office building. "Telegraph service blocked, on strike," he cried excitedly.

"This is the work of the devil!" an infuriated man shouted.

Everywhere were cries of disappointment and anger. Doctor's Nesthäkchen had the most thoughtful face in the world. What should she do now?

"We must get into the city quickly; otherwise we will not find a room in a hotel and will have the pleasure of sleeping at Mother Green's," said a gentleman to his wife, standing close to Annemarie.

A caravan marched along the tree-lined road that wound into the town of Sagan. Annemarie joined the procession. Alone in a hotel in a strange city--as bold as Doctor's Nesthäkchen usually was, this exceptional circumstance weakened her audacity. The concern of her parents lay heavily on her mind, and did not enhance her cheerful courage.

She had almost reached the city, quiet and peaceful in the last evening light. In Annemarie thoughts, violently like a physical pain, flashed a memory, her handbag, the bag with the hundred mark note. Where was it? The people, the trees, the houses began to spin. Icy coldness ran through her veins.

When getting off the train, she held the bag in her hand, definitely. Had she lost it among the many pieces of hand luggage at the station, or in front of the post office? Anyway, she must go back to look for it.

Crowds of people came upon her. "Have you found a small dark green handbag?" How often did Annemarie ask this question over the short distance back to the station? And how often did she receive the same devastating response: "nothing found."

The crowd at the station had dispersed. Searching on the platform was easier. Up and down the young girl ran with boundless agitation but no trace of the green bag. Neither stationmaster nor porters had seen it. It was not in the hand luggage room. Annemarie's last hope vanished.

Night fell. Gold shimmering stars in the dark blue velvet sky silently marked the transition between night and day. Ah, who could now have a roof over her head, a resting place? How happy, how enviable!

Without money at night in a strange city, Doctor's Nesthäkchen did not know where to turn, where to find refuge. The July night was warm. Along the country road was a barn.

Should she crawl in there? No, no, the once brazen girl was suddenly flummoxed.

You dear little gabled room in Arnsdorf: if she were only there. And at home her parents waited in vain. Who could know how long the railroad and postal stoppage would last! How should she spend her life till then?

Wait! Aunt Kate's food package! How fortunate that she had it.

Did she have it? She had given it to the baggage check and gotten a ticket. Where was the ticket? Annemarie fumbled in her coat pockets and in her memory. She could not remember where she put the ticket.

A dark memory: Annemarie had placed the ticket in her green purse. Consequently, she had lost the purse afterward. Or did the official take her hand luggage without issuing a ticket? The crowd had been suffocating. The official would not recognize her. She had to try anyway. Her many comings and goings brought on hunger that the young girl had not felt in her excitement. The backpack contained a lot of food. That was at least a consolation.

O malign fate, the hand luggage office was closed. But the waiting room next to it sent inviting light beams out into the darkness. Should she venture in?

On the benches that ran along the walls of the cavernous room, tired people were huddled, predominantly travelers from the fourth class carriage, who were unable to pay for an expensive hotel.

Annemarie joined them. Most were asleep. Some were engaged in consuming prodigious amounts of food or calming crying children. Annemarie's healthy appetite grew when she saw others eating and had no food for herself. Her blue eyes were covetous.

The common misfortune had created a bond. The passengers chatted with each other and considered the possibility of an onward journey. Annemarie participated in their outspoken conversation. She reported her loss and was greeted with lively compassion. Yes, when they heard that she had filled her backpack with supplies of food and could not retrieve it today, she received small amounts food from all sides. One person handed her a cheese sandwich, another, fruit.

Strangely, Annemarie's gnawing hunger was blown away. How shameful that she had to live on crumbs. Doctor's Nesthäkchen had her pride.

The moon peeped around the corner of the station building. In a foreign environment, if one feels abandoned, the moon is a good friend. He smiled familiarly on Doctor's Nesthäkchen. The heavy hopelessness that had hung on the joyous soul of the young human child crept away. Annemarie bowed her blond head. Gently and evenly her breaths came. She slept amidst the strange environment.

Of course, on awakening, her worries returned. What should she do now? But if you have rested, and the bright day is laughing, everything looks only half as bad. "Oh, I will sell the Arnsdorf eggs and poultry. They surely will bring me so much money that I can spend it on a ticket to Berlin. And if it's fourth class, it's a train. Above all, I must get home."

The other travelers gave her coffee, or pulled out bottles. The teenage girl remembered that she had a bottle of cocoa in her backpack. Nesthäkchen laughed uproariously that Aunt Kate had packed so much food. "I'm not going to America," she had protested. The loving care of her aunt would now serve her in good stead.

Oh, no! The official at the hand luggage counter insisted that he could not give out luggage without a ticket. Otherwise anyone could claim anything. He would make himself liable to prosecution if he did not act according to rules.

Anne Marie's report of the loss of her hand luggage and its contents appeared quite credible. She asked to be allowed to take something to eat from her backpack, since she was so hungry. Nevertheless, the man did not dare to act on his own.

He spoke to the stationmaster. The young traveler described exactly what was contained in the backpack.

Annemarie mentioned a single legged puppet, which Bübchen had thrown in for his "Mie" in the backpack, and which she carried as a souvenir. The stationmaster was impressed by the accuracy of her information.

He delivered a judgment of Solomon: "Your backpack you are allowed to take. The poultry and egg crates stay here. If no one else demands them, you can pick them up in a few days."

"In a few days? How long is the railway strike scheduled to last?" Fearful blue eyes were fixed on the mouth of the official.

He shrugged. "Two weeks, maybe three or four, who knows?"

The young girl saw black before her eyes.

Four weeks she should be stuck here with no money? Aunt Kate's food could pay for a maximum of two days, even with minimal expenses. Annemarie could not sleep in the waiting room every night. There was no help for it: she had to earn money, a sufficient sum for room and board.

Especially for a ticket to Berlin.

Unusually thoughtful, Doctor's Nesthäkchen, the rucksack on her back, plodded off to the city.

What could she do?

Not much. A high school student didn't have significant income potential. One girl in her class tutored younger students. But this activity was not impressively profitable. Tutoring schoolchildren, Annemarie would be unable to feed herself. And you had to have access to students.

Would someone hire her for harvest work? Harvest workers were wanted, she knew from Arnsdorf. But how many times had Peter laughed at her? She had never done hard work. Nope, harvest work was out.

She arrived in town. Sagan was clean and quaint. In the marketplace there was more activity than usual. The reluctant travelers, here against their will, had nothing to do except stroll around. In front of the newspaper store window they gathered together in a blackish knot. They hoped to read about resumption of railway traffic in the daily papers hanging on display.

Annemarie joined the crowd. But she was not interested in the political news. She wanted to read the job ads.

"Wanted" was emblazoned with bold letters as a heading. What was wanted?

"Saleswoman at the Lippold Pastry Shop." That would not be so bad. Mountains of crumb cake and other delicious cakes appeared before Annemarie's eyes. But this job certainly didn't come with a free apartment. And the apartment was necessary for her.

Otherwise not much of the newspaper's content was of interest. What else were they looking for? Young goat, porter, German shepherd, sewing machine, pig trough in good condition, laundress, nanny-- wait, what was that?

Had Cousin Elli not wanted to take Annemarie as nanny with her to Kiel? Had Nesthäkchen not often cared for Bübchen by herself? She could present herself as a nanny with a clear conscience. The duties of a nanny she would be able to satisfy. The best part was that she would receive free room and board. With her earnings she could pay for the return journey to Berlin.

Splendid! Annemarie's heart leaped with bliss. Once more she studied the ad: Looking for nanny, Parkstraße 2. She made her way to try her luck.

Chapter 10.
The Nanny

A tasteful white cottage draped with blue clematis flowers sat in a sunlit garden. It was Parkstraße #2. On the white wooden screen door was attached a porcelain plate, "Dr. med. Waldemar Lange, general practitioner. Office hours 8-10, 4-6 o'clock."

Anne Marie's heart filled with joy a second time. Her lucky star had guided the doctor's child to a doctor's house. If only the place was not too busy!

She pulled the brass bell. The door opened by itself. The path among heavily laden fruit trees and *reseda mignonette* plants led Anne Marie to a stone staircase. Behind the house children's voices were audible, surely her future wards.

At the open front door, Annemarie stood in the hallway in front of a girl with bib apron and white bonnet.

"The doctor's consultation hour is over. You must come back in the afternoon at four," the genie informed her.

Annemarie had to laugh that she was considered a patient.

"I am responding to today's ad to apply for the position of nanny."

"Oh." The girl immediately struck a confidential tone. "It's quite nice here. But the smallest child is terribly unruly. Butter and sugar are included only every fortnight."

"That does not interest me." Annemarie dismissed the confidences with unusual arrogance. Not that it was an insult for the girl in her floral dress to take Nesthäkchen for her peer. On the contrary, she enjoyed it. But she did not like to talk about the man of the house behind his back.

"Come in. You can put your backpack here. If not it's OK. I must go home to my mother. She's sick." The girl opened the door to the balcony room and let Annemarie enter.

On the balcony, looking over the garden, a lady with smoothly cut brown hair was busy trimming children's clothes.

"Madam, here is a would-be nanny answering today's ad," said the girl.

"The young girl can come out to me on the balcony." Friendly brown eyes looked closely at Annemarie.

"Good day, dear child. I need an immediate replacement for my kids' nanny. Are you are free?"

"Yes. I could start right away." Annemarie's heart beat as if it was necessary to pass a final examination.

"Have you references?"

The girl turned pale. She had not thought about the need for references. She had only her school records.

"I was not a professional nanny. I helped with relatives' children," she replied uncertainly.

"Then you do not know how to deal with children?"

"Oh, yes, I have taken care of small children myself. I love little kids." Her blue eyes shone at the lady at reassuringly.

"That is fine for me. And what do you know of housework? "

"I can clean up rooms." She had done that before, when the maid was sick at home.

"What you do not understand, I will show you. You're young and can still learn if you are willing."

"Of that you can be assured," promised the new nanny in-genuously.

"Children's underclothes you need to wash, of course."

"Of course," Annemarie said in agreement although she had no idea how to do that.

"What are your salary expectations?"

Annemarie thought hard: enough to pay for the trip to Berlin. But she could not tell the lady.

"My current girl receives thirty marks a month. I would give you the same thing. If you are satisfied, I will hire you. Is that all right?" asked the lady.

"Yes, definitely." Thirty marks could easily buy a fourth class ticket to Berlin.

"All right, I'll try you, although I otherwise never hire without certificates or inquiries. But I'm in a jam. And I think that I am not mistaken about you. Hopefully we will stay together a long time."

"I hope the opposite, that the railway strike is soon over," thought Annemarie, ashamed that she was deceiving the nice lady. But what was she to do? If she said that she wanted to have the job temporarily, the lady would not hire her. What would she live on?

"Everything is in order. What's your name?"

"Annemarie Braun." Doctor's Nesthäkchen did not want to use an alias.

"How old are you?"

"I will be seventeen soon." She was recently sixteen, but she wasn't lying.

"Where are you from?"

"I'm from out of town, Arnsdorf." She did come from there.

"Do you have relatives in Sagan?"

"No, I'm a stranger here."

"Then you can bring your luggage and move in as soon as possible. My girl is from a village in the neighborhood and would prefer to go home immediately, because her mother is ill."

"I can move in now, ma'am. The essentials I have in my backpack. My luggage is on its way." Again, she was not lying.

The lady was taken aback. Something seemed to be wrong. But she was in a difficult situation and glad to have found a nanny so quickly. Frank and friendly, the young thing had made a good impression. Perhaps a bit too refined, but that was good in dealing with children. From her they would learn nothing bad.

"Then you stay right here, Annemarie. Another thing, you must open the door for patients during office hours and learn to write precise orders for Herr Doktor and use the telephone. It is not too difficult."

"I can do that already," exclaimed Annemarie without thinking.

"How so?" Again the lady was taken aback.

The new nanny blushed to the roots of her curly blond hair. "I helped out at the home of our doctor." Oh God, it was excruciatingly difficult for the honest Annemarie to constantly avoid the truth.

Mrs. Lange was satisfied.

"I'm going to introduce you to your little protegés, Annemarie." The lady descended steps leading from the porch into the garden. The new nanny followed, relieved that she had passed the difficult examination with flying colors.

"So, Rudi and Kätherle, this is your new Annemarie! You will be quite fond of her. "

A lovable two year old girl came up to her mother with short steps. Annemarie began to laugh. The toddler contorted her mouth as if she wanted to cry. But as she looked in Annemarie's merry blue eyes, she began to laugh and shout.

"I'm glad, Annemarie, that our Kätherle goes straight to you. Rudi, our oldest, will soon be ten. Give Annemarie your hand, Rudi. And then there's Edith. Where have you been, girl? Come on, say good day." Around the corner of the arbor peeked a brown curly head, which promptly disappeared.

"We have become friends," said Annemarie, who let Kätherle ride her piggy back, as Bübchen had. Through the whole garden you could hear the shouting. Curious, the brown curly head ventured out again.

"I see, Annemarie, that you know how to deal with children. I leave you with my little company. They have eaten. But you yourself might be hungry?" asked Mrs. Lange in a friendly way.

"Yes, since this morning I haven't eaten anything," Annemarie admitted. "I have sandwiches in my backpack that are not too old."

"Sandwiches?" Rudi laughed. He did not know the word.

"They are cuts," instructed Mother. "But how do you know the Berlin expression, child?"

"I, we have relatives in Berlin who visit us often," said Annemarie embarrassed. She had to cheat once more.

"Take your place in the kitchen with a pot of soup and your sandwiches, Annemarie. Rudi, show Annemarie the kitchen."

"Shaking her head, Mrs. Lange went back into the house. She wondered whether she had done the right thing when she hired the strange girl, of whom she knew nothing. Should she give such a person an intimate place in her house? There was something not quite right. Had she run away from home? But the girl was not bad, certainly. Blue eyes like those could not lie.

The new nanny made the acquaintance of the cook, Auguste, a grumpy lady. Annemarie took her backpack to the nursery, helped her predecessor move out her suitcase, and settled in. It was good that she did not have to live with the cranky Auguste, but should sleep with the children. Auguste would certainly wonder about Annemarie's elegant lingerie.

Mrs. Lange put a freshly washed black satin dress, apron and cap on the table.

"Annemarie, your peasant dress is nice, but Dr. Lange would like our girl to wear black during office hours. I therefore give every new girl a dress, two aprons and two bonnets. If you stay more than a year with us, you are allowed to keep them."

Annemarie had to laugh, because she would hardly get the dress. After Mrs. Lange had left the nursery, she slipped into her new livery.

Oh God, she looked amusing, ready for a masquerade ball. The dress fit excellently; Annemarie was so tall and slender. The skirt was a good fit, too. Mommy liked her to wear an apron at home.

But the bonnet, that was funny, that was truly funny! The new nanny laughed at her handsome reflection in the white bonnet. There were tears in her blue eyes. If only one of the coffee klatsch sisters were here to laugh with her. What would Vera say?

"Oh, Annemarie, you rejoice in your situation. You have probably not seen anything like these clothes at home in your village." Smiling, the returning Mrs. Lange observed the mirth of her nanny. "Can you iron for Kätherle a pair of pants and then go for a walk with the children? Are you accustomed to ironing with gas or iron bolts?"

Ah, the new nanny was not accustomed to ironing. Her clothes, her white blouses and dresses, were impeccably laundered by the maid at home. Mommy had sometimes told her Lotte that she should not be waited on in this way and could iron a blouse quite well herself. But the good Hanne was better at the job and had taken charge of the ironing. No, Doctor's Nesthäkchen did not iron her own clothes. The "child" had enough toil in the form of schoolwork.

"At home, we had an electric iron."

Annemarie had surprised Mrs. Lange once more: an electric iron, how posh. But electric power was cheap in the country, as the power lines reached more of the isolated villages.

"We still iron with a bolt. Auguste is heating it. The ironing board is in the utility room off the kitchen. Auguste will let you know when the bolt is hot."

The new nanny, armed with iron hooks, stood in front of the stove to lift the red hot bolt out of the fire. Oh, if Hanne were here! She could help with the difficult work. Auguste did not move away from her spinach. She provided the necessary instruction, and that was all.

Doctor's Nesthäkchen, otherwise so brave, had a proper fear of glowing bolts that could inflict terrible burns.

Hey there, Anna!" The name Annemarie was too cumbersome for the cook. "The bolt does not bite. Get hold of it," said Auguste after watching at length the futile efforts of the nanny.

Annemarie went for it, because she was secretly ashamed that Auguste should see her awkwardness. Wham! The glowing bolt fell to the flagstone floor, missing Annemarie's feet by a hair and banging into the nickel plated iron. In her fright, the young girl's hand had slipped.

"What a bumpkin! You know nothing," the cook scolded and finally helped bring the matter in order. "The iron got a clunk. I let the Mistress see it."

Ironing is a difficult art for those without the aptitude. The new nanny was ironing the children's pants with an effort that caused bright drops of sweat to bubble up on her forehead. Instead of flattening wrinkles, she was ironing in impressive new wrinkles and fine lines. Kätherle's pants would not be smooth. And what was worst, the snow white linen was turning a brownish color. The vile flat iron was singeing everything. Annemarie spent half an hour ironing the pants. Through the basement window of the utility room that looked out into the garden, the three children peered and wondered whether their new nanny was ready to take them for a walk. Mother had dressed them for their outing. When would they leave?

But the new nanny did not appear. Mrs. Lange rang.

Annemarie was quietly ironing. She did not suspect that the ringing was for her.

The ringing became more insistent. It turned into a storm.

"If you please, will you answer the Mistress' call," cried the surly Auguste from the kitchen. "The kids are ready and will not wait any longer."

Frightened, Annemarie let the pants drop and dashed up the stairs to the living quarters.

"Annemarie, do you have a pair of pants ready? The children must take their walk." Mrs. Lange seemed unimpressed by her new pearl.

Figure 6. Wham! The glowing bolt fell to the flagstone floor, missing Annemarie's feet by a hair and banging into the nickel plated iron.

"I would be done, but they don't look good. I've tried repeatedly." Annemarie had the honesty to own up to her deficiency.

"You do not have experience, child, you will learn" the Mistress said soothingly. "Now quickly, quickly, take the children for their outing."

Kätherle was seated in her white pram.

"Just a moment, I want to take off my apron and put my hat on." The young girl went back into the house.

"But, Annemarie, our nanny always wears an apron and cap. That's what a nanny should wear," said Mrs. Lange firmly. Had she allowed a selfish, vain thing to get into her house?

"Ha ha ha, Annemarie wants to put on a hat like a lady." Rudi laughed at her.

"What a lady!" echoed Edith immediately; even Kätherle joined in the mirth.

"Be well behaved, my pert little company," scolded Mother smiling. "Go with God. Show Annemarie the city park and the oak grove. At a quarter to one, you must be back for lunch, Annemarie. You will hear the factory whistles at twelve."

The new nanny went out amidst her caravan. With Kätherle in the pram, Edith hooked to one arm, Rudi on the other, they strolled the streets of Sagan. Soon they were all good friends. Annemarie quickly overcame the trivial upset involving the bonnet. But when she met her traveling companions from yesterday, the teenage girl dared not raise her eyes.

In Oak Grove Park children were playing ball. Annemarie was a happy child with the other children. She felt sorry when the shrill midday whistle of the factories sounded.

"Do we need a quarter hour to get home?" she inquired of Rudi.

"We can stay a bit longer." Rudi made today's walk with Annemarie pleasant.

But the "bit" was a quarter of an hour and then another. Punctuality had never been the strong suit of Doctor's Nesthäkchen. When Annemarie and her wards reached the market place, it was twelve thirty. They proceeded at a trot down the street. With red faces they arrived home. Mrs. Lange stood glowering outside the gate.

"Annemarie, how unreasonable, the walk should be refreshing for the children. Here they are in the midday heat drenched with sweat. You must undress and wash them. Auguste has set the table. Tomorrow I ask that you are home at the appointed hour. You know, children, how annoyed Father is when he comes from work and can not eat right away." Mrs. Lange did not want to intimidate her new nanny on her first day, so she had turned to the children. But she was dissatisfied. The new nanny did not seem to be reliable.

Annemarie had often received at home a reprimand because of tardiness. But she had shaken it off like a poodle does water. Here at a stranger's house, the situation was different. The rebuke made an impression and sickened her. She wanted to be home on time tomorrow.

The children were washed clean and appeared at table. The host pointed reproachfully at the cuckoo clock. The cuckoo stuck his head out at 1 p.m. Doctor Lange had eaten at 12:30.

"It was so much fun with our new Annemarie, Daddy," Rudi apologized. "She understands how to play ball, and Latin, too."

"What? She understands Latin?" asked the parents with one voice.

"Yes, I repeat every day a page from my Latin grammar, because I got a "C" in Latin. Our new Annemarie has helped me to improve. Isn't that true, Annemarie, you know Latin?" He turned to the girl spooning soup.

In embarrassment she let the soup tureen almost fall to the floor.

"Oh, no no, Rudi," parried Annemarie. "At home were boys, I often had to listen to their lesson." She practically turned her white bonnet red, explaining to the Mistress. The family no longer paid attention to the soup tureen, which they should have been passing around. Slosh! The doctor splashed his soup on his collar and neck.

"Heavens!" Furious, he jumped up. And no one could blame him, because it is not very pleasant in July heat of twenty-six degrees Celsius to feel hot soup running along your back. Mealtime was postponed because Herr Doktor had to change his clothes.

Annemarie wanted to escape as quickly as possible after her masterpiece. But Mrs. Lange said, "You must feed Kätherle, Annemarie. The little one cannot eat her soup alone. But be careful not to repeat the misadventure." The new girl laughed aloud, although she had been depressed. The Silesian expression "Soups" had always tickled the teenage girl's funny bone in Arnsdorf. Surprised she saw the Doctor return to table filled with unseemly mirth.

"You seem to have taken a fourth child into the house, Martha," he said, as Annemarie disappeared with the empty soup bowls. "Where did you find this attractive clumsy girl?"

"She responded to my ad. I do not know if I've done the right thing, to hire her without documents or recommendations. She seems a bit odd. But her eyes make such an honest impression."

"The girl does not seem like an impostor," decided the doctor.

Annemarie brought the spinach. She had to feed Kätherle to prevent green beds from being sowed on the tablecloth. Dr. and Mrs. Lange talked about a piece of art that an acquaintance had bought. It was a black and white drawing. They were not in agreement as to whether the artist was Thoma or Spitzweg.[35]

"The picture is by Thoma," announced the new nanny to her amazed employers. "I know it well." Annemarie broke off abruptly, as a messy green blob graced Kätherle's bib. Annmarie bit her lip. Lord God, her mouth had run away again, as so often before. But the Thoma picture hung at home in her father's room.

---

[35] Josef Thoma (1828-1899) was an Austrian landscape painter. Carl Spitzweg (1808–1885) was a German romantic painter, especially of genre subjects.

"Oops?" said the Mistress. She broke into an amused laugh.

"Did we get an educated girl for our children's nanny?" cried the doctor.

"How do you know the image, Annemarie?" questioned Madame, again suspicious.

"It, it hangs in the consulting room of the doctor, where I worked before." If only they did not want to continue asking questions. Then more came out.

"You worked for a doctor? I like that. What was his name?" the master of the house asked amiably.

"Doctor, Doctor Wohlgemuth." That was the name of a friend and colleague of her father. Annemarie did not feel good about what she had said.

"Where was he?"

"In in in--I have forgotten the name of the place," Annemarie had decided. No, Doctor's Nesthäkchen could not keep lying. She left the bewildered Kätherle sitting with her spinach dish and ran from the room to escape the Doctor's uncomfortable questions and the searching eyes of his wife.

Annemarie was hungry before, not now. She wanted nothing to eat. The dour company of Auguste and the empty kitchen table were not to blame. The excitement about the difficult, complicated situation in which she found herself had robbed Annemarie of her appetite.

When the children had left the room, Mrs. Lange turned to her husband. "Waldemar, did I do right, is this new nanny on the up and up?"

"No, there's something wrong. I noticed the same reticence when she greeted me, and her neat white hands. That she was going to lie is written on her forehead. She is an unspoiled thing, but does not want to tell the truth. What did she bring with her? "

"Virtually nothing, she wore a flowered peasant dress. She had a backpack with her. Her luggage was on the way, she told me."

"I would in any case take the time to investigate her backpack, Martha."

"Oh, Waldemar, I am reluctant to covertly rummage through other people's stuff."

"In this case, it is necessary, child. One must be careful about taking a stranger into the house at the present time. Maybe the backpack has something in it which will give an indication of her personality."

While Annemarie was drying glass and silver in the kitchen, her backpack was subjected by Dr. and Mrs. Lange to a detailed examination. Strange things came to light.

Mrs. Lange pulled out an elegant travel case. "Look, ivory brushes, Waldemar. She either stole this thing, or..."

She did not finish the sentence. Because she had already taken out flower patterned socks, black patent leather shoes and a nightgown with A.B. elegantly embroidered on it. "This is not a simple country girl." Mrs. Lange shook her head. "Here is a book by Lagerlöf."[36]

"Strange reading for a peasant girl," remarked Doctor Lange dryly. "There's another book. What is it?"

"Cicero in Latin. Annemarie Braun, high school student, is written in it. Do you understand what's going on?" Poor Mrs. Lange's head was swimming.

"It seems to me that you have hired a high school student as a nanny, Martha. Rudi has already found that she has knowledge of Latin. She must herself provide us with more clues. Call her in."

---

[36] Selma Ottilia Lovisa Lagerlöf (1858–1940) was a Swedish author. She was the first female writer to win the Nobel Prize in Literature, and is best remembered for her children's book, *The Wonderful Adventures of Nils*.

Annemarie appeared on the double bell rings. She turned pale when she saw spread out on the nursery table the contents of her backpack.

"Do you want to tell us how you got this backpack?" asked the Doctor sternly.

"It's my backpack," was the quiet reply.

"That's impossible. These things belong in all probability to a high school student named Braun. You have appropriated unlawfully not only her possessions, but also her name. I'll take you to the police. They would like to find out who you are and how you come to have these items."

Annemarie saw black before her eyes. Edith's doll carriage, at which she had been looking, began to dance. The police, for God's sake, do not involve them! She had to confess the truth. Everything came out, everything!

"Well?" urged the experienced doctor who saw the internal struggle of the girl.

Annemarie pulled herself together.

"I'm Anne Marie Brown from Charlottenburg. These things really are my property. On the train home to my parents, I got stuck by the railway strike here in Sagan. I lost my purse, which contained all my money. I was forced to take any position to have a place to sleep and avoid starvation. I beg your pardon for deceiving you. I knew no other course of action." Anne Marie's first faltering words became a torrent. It was a blessing to be able to talk about everything from the heart. Certainly the Langes would throw her out.

She felt, to her astonishment, a kind woman's hand. "Poor child," said Mrs. Lange with tears in her eyes. "What you have undergone is unbelievable. If only you had had some confidence in me."

"I had to earn travel money, and I thought I would not get the job if I told you I would be here a short time," explained Annemarie with a relieved conscience.

"Have you notified your parents? Where are they?" asked the doctor.

"It was impossible. The telegraph service was blocked. My parents will be terrified about my disappearance."

"I should think so. Telephone service has been restored. Have your parents a telephone?"

"Of course, ah, if I could give them a ring!"

"What is the number and name?"

Annemarie called out both.

"Braun, Doctor Ernst Braun, Charlottenburg, with whom I studied in Heidelberg?" cried Doctor Lange amazed. "I get the daughter of my old university friend as nanny in my house? Small world."

He immediately rushed to the telephone to make the long distance call.

Soon the worried Doctor Braun knew the whereabouts of his Nesthäkchen. She was safe in Sagan with a former companion of his cheerful student days. Dr. Braun did not understand why Doctor Lange called Annemarie his new nanny. But his main concern was that his child was well cared for until rail traffic resumed.

Yes, Annemarie was surely secure with Dr. Lange in Sagan, no longer as nanny, but as dear foster daughter, with whom Mrs. Lange liked to walk hand in hand. Apron and bonnet were put in storage.

The kids, whom she joyously cared for, loved her. The egg crates and Arnsdorf chicks, at the doctor's intercession, made their way into the Lange household.

But only for a short time: when, after eight days the railway strike was over, Dr. Lange provided Annemarie with travel money. She wished her friends a grateful farewell. They regretted having to say goodbye to the lovely girl. Doctor's Nesthäkchen would have liked to stay with the kindly family, if she had not had to go home to her father and mother.

Chapter 11.
Dance Lessons

The brightly colored daisies in their green flower boxes that Annemarie had planted herself in front of her windows were wilting. November rain beat the last brown leaves dead. Beyond the panes, a blonde girl's head bowed in strenuous work on corpulent folios and folders. She scratched her pen eagerly. From time to time a wrinkle appeared on her white forehead. It was not so easy to advance to the 12th grade. At her high school this period was filled with arduous labor. Doctor's Nesthäkchen, as talented as she was, was forced to strive in order to satisfy the wishes of her teachers.

Three times a week Annemarie was tutoring pupils in the lower classes who had failed to advance. Annemarie's teacher had asked for volunteers. Annemarie Braun and Marlene Ulrich raised their hands immediately. "Just think, Marlene, what struggles we will have deciding how to spend the huge amounts of money we will earn."

Annemarie jubilantly made plans: "Theater and concert tickets, ice rink and tennis. Klaus used his money in the summer to walk with Hans through the Black Forest."

Her parents were not in agreement with their daughter. "Child, you need first to succeed in school. You should do housework during your free time at home; your health will benefit. You saw while working as a nanny for Dr. Lange how little you understand of home economics," said Mother.

"I'll hire myself out as a nanny." Mother's objections made Annemarie laugh. "I'll tutor good students and reject poor students."

"Young girls among the good pupils will have less pocket money than you, Lotte," argued Father. "Forget theater tickets. In today's difficult times you want clothes and shoes. I do not wish for my daughter to take money from needy girls."

"I won't do that, daddy. All those who have come forward have been scheduled. Only weak students have been shut out."

Doctor's mischievous Nesthäkchen morphed three times a week into a respectable teacher and became a mini Croesus, as Father called her jokingly.

One pupil from whom she received no pay gave Annemarie intense pleasure. She taught her friend Vera. The German-Polish girl did badly in her studies. Annemarie mounted a gargantuan effort to make her girlfriend's faulty German immaculate, and to help her overcome the difficulties that grew from lack of understanding of the German language.

Vera's uncle, Herr von Hohenfeld, wanted to take Vera out of school after Easter. "Unnecessary cruelty to animals," he called her classes. Vera should learn printing and photography. But without Vera, high school would no longer be fun for Annemarie. Vera had to advance and stay in school.

The diligent efforts of the girlfriends would surely have been successful if this winter they had not taken dancing lessons. Is it possible to think of German grammar, geometry calculations or irregular verbs, if it is necessary to consider whether, when doing the new dance Hiawatha, one should make three steps left or three steps right? Which turn comes first during the One Step: the grinding turn or the buckling turn? These were matters of such immense importance that you could forget about parallelograms, Virgil or *Hermann and Dorothea*.[37]

Mrs. Braun was against letting Annemarie take dancing lessons this winter. She knew her daughter's short attention span and how easily she could be distracted from her studies. She advised Lotte to wait until after the final examination before beginning dancing lessons.

"Wait until after the exam? By then I'll be an old woman, nineteen years old. No, Mommy, I'll be as stiff-boned as Aunt Albertina. All the girls are taking dancing lessons this winter. If I wait, who knows if Klaus will be studying in Berlin. This year he

---

[37] *Hermann and Dorothea* is an epic poem written by Johann Wolfgang von Goethe between 1796 and 1797.

is still here, just in case. It's good to have a man who will dance with you if there's no one else."

"If you don't graduate, you won't like the dance you need to do, Lotte!"

What good to her daughter are Mother's logic, pleas, and promises? Annemarie took dancing lessons with her girlfriends. She was unafraid to sit down at a dance. The funny, graceful thing was the most popular lady at the dance lesson. Even Vera, who had the light-footed grace of a Polish woman and was, with her delicate face and deep black hair, a beauty, was not as popular as Doctor Braun's lively, childlike, happy Nesthäkchen.

"When Annemarie has her brother Klaus and his friends at the dance lesson, it's no wonder she's constantly in demand," opined the coffee klatsch sisters. But this statement was not entirely free from envy, and therefore not fully relevant.

Annemarie wanted to prove to her mother that she could have dance lessons without neglecting her duties. Indeed, she learned that even if she wracked her brain during intense periods of frenzied studying, she could view tonight's dancing lesson as her reward.

Outside the November rain cozily drummed against the gutter. Annemarie had to write a French essay on Chateaubriand's "Jerusalem."[38] The girls characterized this task as difficult and mind-numbing. *"Les murs de Jerusalem se levent,"* she began, listening to the music of a hurdy-gurdy outside, despite the wind and weather. What was he playing? Oh, Black Forest Girl.[39] Anne Marie's fresh lips began to mouth the familiar tune that sounded up from the courtyard. "La la la la la la la la la la, les murs de Jerusalem se levent sur sept collines tra la la tra la la." Her feet started to tap out the beat. "Les pierres des murs se composent de granit—"

The walls of Jerusalem and Annemarie's sense of duty collapsed at the same time. Her chair flew to the ground. Annemarie jumped between desk and bed in Rhinelander step, up and down. Tra la la la la la.

What did she care which stones composed the walls of Jerusalem? Back and forth she danced, tra la la la la la, right and left, in a circle.

The maid brought the freshly ironed rosebud dress. Astonished, she stopped short in front of the open door, where the young miss was hopping to and fro.

---

[38] Itinerary from Paris to Jerusalem (*Itinéraire de Paris à Jérusalem*) is a travelogue of François-René de Chateaubriand published in 1811. He recounts a trip from July 1806 to June 1807.
[39] Schwarzwaldmädel (Black Forest Girl) is a 1917 operetta in three acts by German composer Leon Jessel.

But Annemarie had already grabbed her. "You know *Black Forest Girl*, Minna, let's dance."

Tra la la la la la!

Minna danced, waving up and down, all around, the freshly ironed rosebud dress in her raised hands.

Tra la la la la, tra la la la la la

Annemarie's zeal for dancing had left Mina no time to hang the dress on the bracket. La la la la la la la la la.

Crack! The concert halted abruptly.

"The doorman, the disgusting Kulicke, has chased the hurdy gurdy man from the courtyard. What a gruff philistine," said angry Doctor's Nesthäkchen. "No matter, we can dance without music. I will sing, Minna."

"Miss Annemarie, I have no time. I have to iron a whole load of clothes." The maid hurried away.

"You must get Hanne." Annemarie's dance mania was inflamed. "Hanne, can you dance the *Jas*?"

"Jas? You must be kidding, Annemiechen! I dance Jas every day during curfews, when I can't cook." Hanne looked like an angry bulldog.

Hanne's protest did not help her. Annemarie grabbed the thick kitchen fairy around her ample waist, while the girl's puckered lips whistled the melody skillfully. Up and down she went with the recalcitrant Hanne, Puck cheerfully barking behind.

"You see, that's the new dance, the Jas, Hanne. All young maidens under fifty must learn it."

"May the devil take modern dances! At almost seventeen, you're still acting like a kid, Annemiechen. Aren't you ashamed? How can Minna have the proper respect for you?" scolded Hanne. As punishment Annemarie whirled her around in a gallop. "This dance will soon be old fashioned for you, Hanne!" With that she let the portly Jas dancer return to her kitchen.

"Stick with your books," snarled Hanne breathlessly.

"Is this the seriousness that you need for your work?" rang out from the next room reproachfully. Mother was resting, and the noise had disturbed her.

Annemarie crept back to her desk ashamed, Puck to his basket. Who could help it if suddenly an organ grinder caused her to cast all her good intentions to the four winds? Annemarie delved back into her French essay. But she could not prevent the Black Forest Girl from peeking between the walls of Jerusalem every now and then.

Seven strokes boomed from the grandfather clock. Whap! Annemarie slapped her book shut. It was time to dress. Today she had to look particularly fine. Grandma and Brother Hans, who was studying this semester in Berlin, had promised to come and watch the dance lesson.

"Is our lady ready for the ball?" Dr. Braun, who was sitting at the dinner table, looked at his pretty daughter with paternal pride.

"Yes, but Klaus is whining. He has been running around a whole hour with a mustache bandage and thinks it will make his cute peach fuzz grow. I want to tack a caution sign on his mustache.

"Wise apple!" Her arriving brother interrupted her spray of words. "As punishment, I will not dance a single time with you today."

"O God, you will not do this to me, Kläuschen. Then I must play wallflower and decorate the wall for the whole evening," laughed the demon.

"You deserve it!" Klaus looked, in his dark blue suit, a handkerchief corner impudently poking from the left breast pocket, no less elegant than his attractive sister. Since October he was a student at the Agricultural College.

"What, Klaus, now you want to eat? It is already five minutes to eight, and I was asked to judge the first one-step," said Annemarie.

"The unhappy dancers must be patient. My cheese sandwich is more important to me."

"Lotte, you eat too little. You're not leaving without supper," said Father.

"I can not, Daddy, I'm terribly tired."

"In the country we call it ball fever," laughed Hans, her best brother. "Come, little one, I feed you."

"Lotte, do not forget to put on a dressing gown over the dress. The gown is darkly lined and can be cleaned. And overshoes in this weather!" Mother knew her reckless girl would prefer to run out as she was.

"Margot is gone. I heard her door close. We always arrive late," said Annemarie.

Minna pulled one overshoe on her, Hanne the other. Hans pushed a supper morsel into her mouth. There was excitement in the whole house before a dancing lesson.

"I can not breathe, Mommy." The teenage girl fought back when Mother wrapped a precautionary head scarf around her neck.

"Goodbye."

"Goodbye."

"Do not get overheated, my girl."

The Braun cloverleaf was out the door and down the stairs.

"Peace has returned to the land." The parents breathed a collective sigh of relief.

"Whew! What weather," Annemarie shivered in the pattering rain.

"Do we want to turn back?" teased Hans.

"Yes, yes, says Olja." Cocky Annemarie wrapped her arms around one brother on her left, the other on her right, and plunged forth.

The dance class was held in a social hall. An amiable young lady, Miss Steinert, gave the lessons. The girls swooned for her, and the young men longed.

Pleasantly warm, the illuminated vestibule welcomed the three soaked siblings. Latecomers were crowding the cloakroom.

In the hall dance music was playing.

"Quick, quick, it has already begun." Annemarie tore off headscarf and coat as her cavalier appeared.

"Why did you come so late? We learn the Boston today, Annemarie." The cavalier pulled his partner into the hall. The radiant glow of light bulbs bathed the white, pink and pale blue garbed girls and their partners, most in knickerbockers, hopping up and down. By the walls were the various mothers and aunts, armed with lorgnettes, who eagerly noted whether their daughter or niece was dancing less frequently than a girlfriend. In their midst Annemarie saw Grandma's sweet face.

Music, bright lights, hot girls' cheeks, waving hair, and Miss Steinert's commanding voice. Annemarie swam in a sea of bliss. She nodded beaming to Grandma while executing a slow grinding turn. But what was that? Grandma nodded, but not so friendly as usual. In painful embarrassment she waved to her granddaughter. And the other ladies? They had raised their lorgnette glasses and were on their feet. What was there for them to stare at? Annemarie squinted at Fritz Richter's pant leg passing her feet. Good heavens, she had not taken off her overshoes. Between all the glowing gold spangled dancing shoes, the dirt-covered monsters jumped around like clumsy giants among a crowd of graceful elves. Her feet had such a strange feeling. But it would be stupid to stop the dance in the middle. The rubber overshoes were not bad for the abrasive turns of the One-step. And the lorgnettes all around hardly disturbed Annemarie's pleasure. When they became accustomed to the appearance of her elegant footwear, they would look elsewhere.

Amidst the heap doing the One-step, a spoiler came. A hand that belonged to brother Hans lay on her arm and held her tight.

"Annemie, you must stop dancing immediately. You're mortifying Grandma and shaming yourself in front of these strange women. You must strip off your elephant shoes and the Flying Dutchman grasping your shoulder." He began laughing at the strange ball dress of his sister.

"What shall I do, Hans?" Annemarie let go of Richter. As she grabbed her shoulders an odd object fluttered down.

"Lord God, my dressing gown! That's what happens when you have to wear such a stupid thing! Who can remember it in a hurry? One moment and the damage will be cured." Untroubled by the stalking eyes following her and the astonished eyes of couples dancing past, Doctor's Nesthäkchen, in the middle of the room, got rid of her Flying Dutchman and the elephant shoes, to the strains of One-step.

The ladies at the walls smiled. Grandma smiled likewise, albeit her grin was forced. As a graceful butterfly emerged from her caterpillar vestments and merrily flew about the dance floor, the mothers had to concede that Dr. Braun's youngest was the most elegant among all of the floating elves.

Good Brother Hans trotted with dressing gown and over-shoes to the coat check, muttering amused to himself: "such a crab!"

The dance was over! The boys retreated to a corner of the hall, the girls opposite. There was whispering and giggling.

"Annemie, why don't you wear slippers to dancing class?" teased Ilse.

"How can anyone be so forgetful?"

"Of course, nothing like that can happen to the virtuous sheep."

"You looked like a huge bat fluttering around the hall," laughed Vera. Annemarie went over to Grandma to escape the derision of her coffee klatsch sisters.

Grandma, loving and good, had overcome the embarrassment into which she had been plunged by Annemarie's carelessness. She stroked her favorite's exuberant curly blonde hair from her hot forehead and handed her a bulging bag of sweets to cool herself and her girlfriends. Grandma insisted she did not know anything of the new dances. Waltz, polka, Rhinelander, quadrille and contra, dances of her youth, were much nicer.

Anne Marie's impressive bag of candy attracted the young men, under the leadership of Klaus, out of their corner. In the middle of their feasting rang out the hand-clapping of Miss Steinert: "Three couples to do the Boston."

Three youths pounced on the expectant girls and snagged three of them. Among them, of course, was Annemarie Braun, who was always bound to be chosen.

Miss Steinert danced the steps and turns. "Always against the beat you loop, the opposite of the waltz. The first pair, please."

Klaus and Vera stepped forward.

"One two three four five six, one two three, wrong, make a reverse step, Mr. Braun," cried Miss Steinert.

"Mr. Braun" made the reverse step and emitted a pitiful cry, "Oh my foot," drowning out the sounds of the Boston. Vera had leaped in a circle like a white wagtail on his foot, while Annemarie lovingly shouted "camel."

"Complete; the second pair."

Marlene was with a young man who was known for his uncanny height to the boisterous lasses as "the Infinite." Marlene, small, petite, could not reach up to his shoulder. She clung firmly somewhere above his elbow as they started to dance.

"One two three four."

The Infinite lost his tiny lady somewhere between dance steps. Everyone made her own strange jumps that resembled more the zoo than the Boston.

The third pair stepped forward. Annemarie's partner was a nice schoolboy, about as musical as a haddock. The girl tried to make herself invisible as soon as he appeared, because it was impossible to get into step with him.

He worshiped Annemarie Braun. The coffee klatsch sisters giggled and gleefully taunted as the wretch sailed toward Annemarie.

Miss Steinert counted. "One two three four five six."

Annemarie Braun counted more loudly. "One two three four five six."

At every number she struck with her left hand the shoulder of the unmusical dancer. The trick succeeded. The couple danced to the beat, and did their job well. However, next day the cavalier's right shoulder was bruised. Annemarie had learned boxing from Brother Klaus ages ago.

One pair after another came forward, one skillful, the next clumsy, until all had danced. They repeated the dances they had already learned. Waltz, polka and Rhinelander were unearthed from oblivion, to grandmother's reassurance.

"Women's choice." This was an exciting proposition for the young men. Would a flaming teenage girl enliven the dancing lessons by curtseying before a swain? Would she skip him and choose another? Seven young men's hearts beat faster as Annemarie's rosebud dress hopped forward. Alas, it hopped on, past an entire row of self-conscious boys, to the mothers and aunts by the piano, leaning on which was brother Hans. Doctor's Nesthäkchen sank into a deep curtsy. "May I ask you for this dance, sir?"

"No, Annemie, you can not demand that I carry my mossy head among the jumping lambs. Look at those zavaliers sitting there with longing eyes.

When she was a tiny girl, Annemarie pronounced *cavalier* as *zavalier* and Hans never forgot.

Annemarie ignored his refusal. She wanted no other "Zavalier." Hans had to dance Hiawatha with her, followed by the envious eyes of her seated admirers. Annemarie beamed. No one was as fine a dancer as her Hans, who was good at everything he did.

The dance lesson was over. The sweating piano player packed up his music. In the hall, the teenage girls crowded around Miss Steinert: "Oh please, please can we dance a little more?"

The nice young lady smiled kindly.

"If someone will play the piano."

Yes, there was the catch. Neither the girls nor the boys wanted to assume that duty. All of them wanted to dance.

"Hänschen has to play. Hänschen plays fine!" Annemarie rushed to her brother and after her the whole swarm of dance maniacs.

"Hänschen must play, oh, please, please," all cried. Hans could not resist the pleas of so many beautiful eyes. They dragged him in triumph to the piano.

We want to dance the Basket. We want to dance the Basket," everyone cried.

"What is that?"

"You'll see. Where do we get baskets?" Several girls rushed into the dressing room in vain. A basket could not be found.

Annemarie and Vera had the good idea to ask in the kitchen downstairs. One came back with a huge market basket, the other with a laundry basket.

"Children, should we dance with those?"

"It must be a small dainty cup," said a young girl.

"We don't have one, so it must be a market basket."

One of the ladies was put into a chair, and the market basket passed gracefully into her hands. Two gentlemen came before her and bowed. One got the basket; with the other she danced away laughing. But the gentleman who received the basket had to sit on the chair. Two ladies curtsied before him. Now he could dispose of his basket and float away with the lucky girls. So it went, blow for blow, and given the size of the basket, the dance game was especially amusing.

The girls were not ready to go home. Mothers waved. Fathers and ministering spirits, who had appeared to pick them up, yawned. Grandma narrowed her eyes. But the laughter and dancing seemed endless.

The host took pity on the weary wall decorations. He turned off the electric light. He had rented the room for two hours only.

Commotion and a cheer broke out.

Vera could not find her aunt, Marianne tumbled into the wash basket, and Annemarie danced by herself in the Egyptian tomb-like darkness as the dance came to end. Had a happy mother snatched her chick, next moment the chick would have escaped in the dark.

Finally, everyone repaired to the dressing rooms, a tangle of overshoes and legs.

"Children, did you finish your French essay on Jerusalem?" asked Marlene, as she looped her pink silk scarf around her dark hair.

"Nonsense, tomorrow there is still time"

"Today we do not think of the stupid school."

Anne Marie laughed: "Yes, sur les murs de Jerusalem nous dansons Boston et Foxtrot."[40]

Grandma tenderly embraced her dancing Doctor's Nesthäkchen. Under the open umbrella, they danced the Boston home through the rain-soaked streets. The old lady had to ignore the splashing puddles. Her granddaughter was uncontrollable. In her nightgown, Annemarie danced into bed, and from there went on to badminton..

---

[40] On the walls of Jerusalem we dance Boston and Foxtrot.

Chapter 12.
Coal Shortage

It was cold, bitterly cold. A northeasterly wind whistled and howled in the oven. There he was able to enjoy himself to his heart's content, because in many Berlin ovens there was no fire. The coal shortage was acute in the city.

In Nesthäkchen's formerly cozy parlor, flower-like frost patterns appeared on the window panes instead of colorful morning glories and daisies.

It was no longer comfortable. Bitter cold it was in Annemarie's kingdom. "Greenland" Annemarie had christened it. The scant coal available had to be used for heating the consulting room and the living room.

Between the white flowered crib and the bed with its rose-colored quilt, an Eskimo with rose red nose marched back and forth. She was wearing a fur coat and fur overshoes on her feet, as if, instead of the carpet, a meter high snow drift lay there. A thick green woolen toboggan cap was pulled low over her ears and covered all her unruly blond hair. A green wool scarf was wrapped several times around her neck and reached up to her rose red nose, which was emitting clouds in second long intervals. It was so cold in the room that you could see her breath. The hands of the Eskimo were in huge mittens, which belonged

250

to the winter sports equipment of her eldest brother. They seized a volume of Tacitus like two mighty bear paws. And if the radiant blue eyes over the rose colored nose had not been visible, no one would have recognized Doctor's Nesthäkchen in her Eskimo garments.

Back and forth the fur shoes went, softly up and down. The icy temperature made it impossible to sit at the desk. Amidst the breath clouds, elegant Latin phrases rolled through the mesh of green toboggan scarves. The Eskimo was so engrossed in reading Latin that she did not notice the door opening behind her.

"Lotte, poor worm! You will freeze. Go to your mom, Annemiechen, in the living room. It is nice and cozy." Hanne's blue red face was filled with compassion as she observed the freezing Eskimo.

"Nope, that will not do, Hanne, too much hullabaloo. I can't learn Tacitus." Her voice sounded muffled through the layers of wool.

"Hullabaloo? You're mistaken, child. Mrs. Braun is the quietest woman in the world, if you yourself are creating no hullabaloo."

"You do not understand, Hanne. Down there my canary Antics sings and warbles. Mommy's scissors and her thimble are always falling down. Klaus comes in and starts pounding to resole his boots. Every few minutes the phone rings. For Tacitus you need absolute peace and the ability to collect your thoughts.

"I care more about freezing than *Tacitussen*," growled the kitchen fairy, annoyed that Nesthäkchen would not listen to reason. "Drink the hot beer that I cooked for you, child." She set a steaming cup on the table. "If you heat yourself internally, you need not heat yourself externally."

"Hanne, you're the very best, but you are a complainer. I have something that's better for heating you up than warm beer and coal." In her bear paws the Eskimo grabbed the unsuspecting Hanne and began to grind through the room in a lively fox trot step.

"Annemiechen, you're completely crazy," gasped the portly Hanne breathlessly. "Dance a fox trot for my sake with Tacitussen, but, if you please, include me out." She slammed the door behind her.

The Eskimo laughed like a goblin behind her. Then she set upon the hot beer. She felt quite cozy thereafter. A few more times she beat her arms around her body, the way Berlin carriage drivers did. Refreshed, she went back to work.

The bell was not quiet during office hours. Hand in hand with the cold, flu, the insidious disease that wiped out so much flourishing human life, made its way through the streets of the city. There was hardly a house that had been spared the evil visit. The doctors had no rest day or night. And Doctor Braun, in his tireless devotion to duty, allowed himself almost no time for meals.

"You're working yourself to death," warned his worried wife.

"For eating and drinking there must be time. If not, you don't need to blame the devil if you end up falling on your nose," grumbled Hanne. She repeatedly had to pack away heated food because sick people in need of help kept showing up.

Annemarie asked her father, with a tender caress, to get more rest. But neither the worries of his wife, Hanne's buzzing, or Nesthäkchen's cajoling were sufficient to prevent Doctor Braun from letting up on his unceasing obligation. His strict sense of duty was, without his knowing it, an example for his children worth copying.

Hans, the eldest, didn't need it. As a schoolboy Hans was always first in all his classes. He passed his exams with distinction and was now, as a trainee, just as efficient and hardworking as he had been as a student.

With Klaus, however, the case was different. Klaus had always obeyed the aphorism: "If you don't try to get out of work, you're crazy."[41] Through high school he had happily swindled his way with breathtaking skill, cheating and using mnemonics. How he breezed through his classes and managed to graduate was, in the Braun family, an unsolved mystery. Nobody had seen him study for his final examination. His college years were no different: drinking, carousing, truancy. He frittered away the first few semesters. But now that he saw his father working day and night in the service of humanity, he began to feel ashamed of his sybaritic life. He no longer went on beer sprees with his pals. He appeared not only as a guest but as a regular listener at the college. At home he soled boots for the whole family, including Hanne and Minna, although no one could run in them because somewhere a treacherous nail stuck out.

His beneficent employment meant more noise in the house and was the cause of discord between him and his sister. Annemarie was full of ingratitude, disturbed by the heinous hammering while trying to learn. Klaus for his part asserted that the mildest man could go stark raving mad in the presence of Annemarie's loud efforts at memorization.

Annemarie's attitude was "full steam ahead" despite the cold. She must be diligent to be able to study medicine and to

---

[41] "Wer die arbeit kennt und sich nicht drückt, der ist verrückt."

relieve Father, who was always willing to help a patient regardless of his own health. If she had such a goal in front of her, selfish desires were silenced. Her ice skates could flash and sparkle, until it was time to do homework. As for her sled, the pleasure of its use was reserved for Sunday in Grunewald. Even her dance lessons, with all their magic sounds, she pushed, summoning all willpower, into the background as long as textbooks led the regiment. "If I am wracking my brain, I do not notice the cold," joked Annemarie.

One of Nesthäkchen's pupils had fallen victim to the cold. Vera's building was on strike. Her apartment, which had central heating, had no heat for weeks because of the lack of coal. Whenever tenants complained they were threatened and cursed; complaining did them no good. They had to freeze.

Anne Marie's "Greenland" was not warmer. The family room, which mother made available to the young girl, was rejected because it was the center of all domestic noise. Annemarie proposed to relocate the tutoring session to a lake, the Neuer See, which weeks ago had been transformed into a mirror-like ice rink. With enthusiasm Vera accepted. Vera was a fantastic ice skater, as was Doctor's graceful Nesthäkchen. Yes, yes on the frozen lake you were warm. It was an excellent spot for teaching and learning. Teacher and student brought good will along. If only there had been a dance band so that the girls could practice the new dances they had learned in their dance class. But could they study dry grammar when their legs jumped to perform an elegant ice dance, which aroused the admiration of the spectators on the snow covered banks. In the middle of a scholarly dispute, some student from the dance class would appear, and the whole of German grammar, which Annemarie had so painfully tried to instill into Vera's pretty head, was cast aside.

Vera's advancement prospects in school were bad. If only the cold and the coal shortage were to blame.

This winter, the girls went willingly to school. There you warmed yourself, at least. The municipal authorities were sufficiently supplied with coal.

One day a surprise was waiting. Mr. Lustig, the singing teacher, taught the first class because no light was needed to sing. He told the students that his class would be held today for the last time in the Lyceum. The neighboring boys' school would henceforth be used by the female high school students. Their classes would be taught in the afternoon from two to seven o'clock. In this way, the heat would be twice utilized, halving the school's coal consumption.

"Fine, we can at least sleep late!" Annemarie Brown said enthusiastically.

Figure 7. In Grunewald excitement and happy activity prevailed. Sledding, the girlfriends forgot coal shortages and unheated rooms.

"My father is in court in the morning. I can do my home-work in his warm office," exulted Marlene.

"Me too."

"Me too."

There was joy over the change. However, there were also some objecting voices: "That is not possible; I have gym class twice a week in the afternoon."

"We have our book discussion groups on Saturday after-noon."

"My piano lesson can certainly not be moved."

"Our dance lesson begins at six clock; we can't miss that."

In spite of gymnastics and piano lessons, despite reading groups and dancing lessons, the authorities had no mercy. Edu-cation took place in the afternoon.

"The Eskimo from Greenland may relocate," explained Nesthäkchen at home. A day later, after Father's morning office hours, she confiscated his pleasant warm rooms.

Doctor Brown was not thrilled. He liked his kingdom for himself. Mommy tried to maintain order, especially on his desk.

But he claimed that everything had been moved and that he could not find anything. Now that his scurrying Nesthäkchen had broad access to his sanctuary, she was worse than ever. His prescription pad and record book were who knows where? Today, the stethoscope was not in its place, tomorrow a forgotten French book peeked out among the medical journals.

"If you can't keep your thoughts and your stuff together, you march back to Greenland, understood, Lotte?" Doctor Brown threatened his youngest and laughed at his words.

"Before my frost bite is cured, you must not throw me out, Daddy. Otherwise I will get the flu!" The sly girl knew how worried her father was that his youngest could become ill in her unheated room.

Mommy worried more. She knew that Annemarie, in her husband's warm consulting room, could easily ingest the threatening flu bacilli that floated around.[42] Half of Annemarie's school class was sick.

---

[42] Influenza is caused by a virus, not a bacillus. The first influenza virus to be isolated was from poultry, when in 1901 the agent causing a disease called "fowl plague" was passed through Chamberland filters, which have pores that are too small for bacteria to pass through. The cause of influenza, the Orthomyxoviridae family of viruses, was first discovered in pigs by Richard Shope in 1931. This discovery was followed by the isolation of the virus from humans by a group headed by Patrick Laidlaw at the Medical Research Council of the United Kingdom

The teachers were ill, too. All had to pay tribute to the disease that was in fashion.

"We are immune, Mommy. In a doctor's house, the flu does not dare enter. "Presente medico nihil nocet," boasted Nesthäkchen with her Latin skills.[43]

But the flu, always insidious, took no account of Anne Marie's Latin scholarship. It slipped unseen up the red runner on the stairs. Returning from school, Annemarie scurried into the Thielen apartment. There she saw Margot with burning forehead on her sickbed. Margot's little brothers and sisters were sick as well. Doctor Braun visited the Thielens, three times on some days, to look after the seriously ill family, especially Margot, whose fever was alarmingly high. If Annemarie asked her father about her girlfriend, he shrugged his shoulders. She was very bad.

Annemarie had no desire to study, skate or dance. Standing pressed against the window, staring at the Thielens' apartment, her breath melted peepholes in the flowering ice crystals.

---

in 1933. However, it was not until Wendell Stanley first crystallized tobacco mosaic virus in 1935 that the non-cellular nature of viruses was appreciated. No one knew this fact when Else Ury was writing in 1919.
[43] In the presence of a doctor nothing can harm.

The Thielens' windows were not frozen, because they were less exposed to the sharp east wind. From time to time, a white nurse's cap appeared at the window. Annemarie's heart beat faster. How was Margot? Dear God, would she die? Annemarie had no true idea of how sick her girlfriend was.

Had Annemarie not often made fun of Margot's pedantic ways? Had she not coined the name "virtuous sheep?" And how many times she had tenderly embraced, caressed and hugged Vera, merely to make Margot jealous. If only she could atone for her sins.

Gladly would Annemarie have personally looked in on the poor Margot. But Nesthäkchen's parents had strictly forbidden any communication with the Thielens for fear of contagion.

The flu cared less than Nesthäkchen about parental prohibitions. Through the back door, it ventured into the Braun kitchen. Minna, the housemaid, was the first to be taken into its clutches. Hanne cared for her faithfully and puffed up her chest: "The flu will always remain three steps away from me. I'm not such a pushover."

It really seemed as if the flu had respect for the resolute Hanne. It made a wide berth around the energetic kitchen fairy and stretched its bony finger to the slender woman with prematurely graying hair standing at the living room window.[44]

Mommy was sick. Every child feels discomfort when her mother, who is there for everyone, must stay in bed. Annemarie suffered this discomfort to an alarming degree.

She was not allowed to visit Mother, who could not care for her or keep her company. The girl's heart ached. Yes, they even sent her out of the house. Mommy had arranged it. For young people the flu was more dangerous than for the old. Mrs. Braun did not rest until her youngest moved with a small suitcase to Grandma's apartment. Annemarie was forced to comply with Mother's wishes, so as not to increase her fever.[45]

Since Annemarie was young, visiting Grandma was like a holiday. Grandma's home was so peaceful, so bright and clean, filled with ancient mahogany furniture, blooming tulips and hyacinths on all the windows with their snow white tulle curtains. Grandma herself was enticing, always friendly; she understood childish wishes.

---

[44] Else Ury has transposed the devastating Spanish Flu pandemic, winter 1918-1919, which claimed 50 million lives worldwide, to winter 1919-1920.

[45] Influenza is ordinarily most lethal for the very young and very old. A characteristic of the Spanish Flu epidemic, 1918-1919, was that a significant proportion of fatalities were people in the prime of life.

This time, Annemarie did not feel as well as usual in the cozy rooms. The good grandmother cooked her all her favorite dishes and used her chattering knitting needles quietly, so as not to disturb her granddaughter's studying. But Grandma could heat one room, and even that only for a few days.

Annemarie had neither the desire to work or to be entertained. That was odd in the lively granddaughter, whose cheerful presence Grandma usually found refreshing.

"Child, are you healthy? Is anything wrong? No limbs aching, no chills?" The old lady inquired with the anxiety of a Grandmother many times a day.

Annemarie laughed her fresh laugh, but not for long. She was quiet and withdrawn. Maybe if she had Mommy! Mrs. Braun was tender and vulnerable after her internment during the first year of the war in England. Not without reason, the young girl worried that the weak health of her mother would not allow Mommy to survive the flu. Every morning, Annemarie crept home across the yard into the kitchen.

"Hanne, how's Mom?" Nesthäkchen's blue eyes were fearful.

"Tut, tut, tut, child, I cook you up a pigeon soup. But you must leave right after. If our doctor catches you here, there will be a thunderstorm."

Bam! The door slammed, locking out Annemarie with all her anxiety and the thousand questions that were still burning in her mind about her mother. As she stood in front of the closed door she felt the same as Puck, who was not allowed in the sick room.

At the Thielens the danger had passed. There was at least a ray of hope. Margot's fever had abated but she expected a long stay in bed, because her lung was involved slightly. Annemarie wrote her tender letters to delight her and salve her own conscience.

"Tomorrow we have to stay in bed, Annemiechen," opined Grandma one day to her astonished granddaughter.

"Oops, the darn flu has infected you?"

"A preventive measure: Today we put the last coal in the furnace. Every day I am reassured by the coal dealer that he will get in more coal. But I can not freeze, for that I am too old. Consequently, we stay in bed." Grandma was dead serious.

"Me too, Granny? I put on my Eskimo uniform again. I am becoming accustomed to Greenland temperature," interjected Annemarie energetically.

Throughout the day they rehashed the idea that poor grandma might freeze solid tomorrow. The old lady sat in the heated room in her crocheted sweater. How could they get coal?

When Annemarie came home to Grandma from school that evening with cold reddened cheeks, a second guest was in residence: Aunt Albertina with nightgown, toothbrush, curlers, bag and baggage.

"Aunt Albertina, you dare to emerge into cold, eighteen degrees, from your warm room? You're otherwise not so adventurous," said the teenage girl with surprise.

"Child, if I had a warm room, wild horses couldn't drag me out. But I'm freezing for three days. I feel tearing in my bones." Aunt Albertinchen's poodle locks hung down sadly, with no sign of their funny wiggle. "I know that Grandma has an empty bed for me, so I decided to relocate here. I had no idea that the bed was already occupied, and that it is as cold here as at my place."

"Aunt Albertina, today we still have heat. It is quite cozy here."

"Yes, but tomorrow! Tomorrow I'll be as frozen here as at home. Oh, who would have told me in my youth that I would be so cold again in my old age."

Aunt Albertinchen's cares did terribly touch Annemarie's loving heart. Nesthäkchen slept on the sofa at night because the bed was, of course, assigned the old auntie with the carefully coiled curls. Annemarie racked her brain: Where could they scrounge coal for the two old ladies. Unrestful dreams about coal plagued the young sleeper. Agitated, she threw herself back and forth on the unfamiliar sleeping accommodations.

Bang! Loud banging, clanking, startled exclamations.

"Merciful heavens, are there burglars?" Aunt Albertina whispered. Her curls stood on end with horror.

Grandma's heart pounded with fear. "Child, Annemiechen what's the matter, what happened?" With trembling hands, she turned on the electric light.

Doctor's Nesthäkchen sat in her nightgown on the floor between sofa and table. She laughed and laughed.

Drinking glass and water jug, which she had knocked from the table, lay in shards nearby.

"What happened, Granny? I dreamed that I got coals for you, a whole basket full. But an electric train came, and I wanted to get out of the way to avoid being run over. That's when I slipped. Oh, it's funny, it's funny." Nesthäkchen held her sides with laughter.

"So, no burglar, thank God." Aunt Albert gradually calmed down.

Grandma was concerned. "Have you hurt yourself, Anne-miechen? Did you break anything?"

"Nothing but the carafe and the drinking glass," was Annemarie's lively reply. "But when I slipped I lost all the coal I had found for you. Terrible!" Annemarie crawled back into her couch-bed.

She did not fall asleep quickly. Hissing and puffing came from Aunt Albertinchen as she slept. From the other corner Grandmother whistled melodiously in her slumber. What a snoring a duet!

Annemarie could not rest. The thought pursued her: Where could she get coal? She had had so much in her dream.

Next morning there was not a single piece of coal in grandmother's home. The two old ladies had coffee in bed, because outside it was uncomfortably cold. The thermometer showed more than twenty degrees of cold.

"Oh, Annemiechen, do not sleepwalk again. You gave me an awful fright. I could not go back to sleep," Grandma yawned.

"Granny, you whistled like a bullfinch. A beautiful snore concert you and Aunt Albertinchen performed," said the granddaughter laughing.

"That must have been Aunt Albertina. I was happily sleeping until dawn."

Aunt Albertina claimed not to have closed her eyes the whole night. She could sleep only in her own bed.

"Then I must have snored cheerfully by myself." Annemarie was amused.

"I want to see if the central heating at the Burkhards is working. I can study there with Vera." Annemarie clapped her fur cap to her blond hair.

"Child, you should stay in a warm bed. You are seeking God, trying to leave in such cold," protested Grandma.

"The flu is so widespread. You will be sick before you know it," chimed in Aunt Albertina.

But the teenage girl laughed off the concerns of the old ladies. Why in broad daylight should she go to bed? She was healthy. No, that was not for Doctor's Nesthäkchen. You froze only at home, if you crouched behind the stove. Outdoors the cold drove the blood more quickly through your veins, as if it was warm. So claimed the greenhorn, as she happily pulled on her muffler and left the house.

It was not warm in the street. The cold stung like needles. Pedestrians had coats or fur collars turned up above their ears. They tripped as though walking on a glacier. Thousands of ice crystals flashed and glared.

Doctor's Nesthäkchen went first to her parents' apartment. She had to hear if her mom had a good night, and if she
was doing better.

She did not venture up the front steps, for fear of being
caught by her father. In the yard, the caretaker was about to
unload coal from a handcart. His young adopted son, Annemarie's special friend, helped him.

"Maxie, where did the coal come from?" Annemarie
looked with covetous eyes at the black lumps, as if they were
made of chocolate.

"We found it."

"How, Max?"

"I won't tell you." The boy jumped with delight or cold
from one leg to the other.

"Max, I've got a sweet for you." Annemarie fished with
frozen fingers in her pocket.

The boy made covetous eyes.

"Where is it? You don't have anything. You're trying to
swindle me," he said naughtily.

Annemarie could not find the candy. She had probably
eaten it herself.

"Maxie, I'll bring you tomorrow a whole bag full, if you tell me where you got the coal," promised the young girl.

Instead of answering, the villain turned up his nose and was gone inside the doorman's apartment.

What a brat, on whom she had once settled the noble name of Hindenburg.[46] She had striven and sewn diapers by hand for this rascal, when Hans brought him home years ago, a war-orphaned infant from East Prussia. Ingratitude is the world's reward!

She had to ask the caretaker himself about coal. Maybe he had left over a few lumps for Grandma. Hanne had helped Grandma out quite a few times but could give no more away. Otherwise father's office and the sick room of Mother would remain unheated.

"Oh, Mr. Kulicke," asked Annemarie when the man appeared in the courtyard in order to store a new load, "where do you get coal?"

---

[46] Paul Ludwig Hans Anton von Beneckendorff und von Hindenburg, known universally as Paul von Hindenburg (2 October 1847 – 2 August 1934) was a German military officer, statesman, and politician who served as the second President of Germany during the period 1925-1934.

The caretaker was denounced as a ruffian by the tenants. But Doctor's Nesthäkchen and her radiant blue eyes had a way with him like no one else.

"Well, Miss, because it's you: I carted the coal from Nordhafen at the crack of dawn. We won't have a drop of coffee tomorrow."

"Oh, dear Mr. Kulicke, could you not spare me a few coals?" begged Annemarie. "My grandmother has to stay in bed today because she has no heat."

"We have been cold for days. Only the rich can have heat."

Father was right: This Kulicke was surely a Spartacist, thought Annemarie. Nevertheless, she tried for salvation again.[47]

"We would pay you well, Mr. Kulicke, if you would procure for us a cart full of coal."

"If you want to have coal, get it yourself, if you please. The rich think they can buy anything with money. No! Those days are over. You will not feel the cold when you haul a coal load like this one. Let's see how you sweat. Ha ha ha."

---

[47] The Spartacists, led by Rosa Luxemburg and Karl Liebknecht, were a group of radical socialists who found fame in the first few months after the November 1918 Armistice when Germany experienced its so-called Revolution. The Spartacists were named after Spartacus who led a revolt by slaves against the might of the Romans in 73 B.C.

The man laughed scornfully.

"I'd like to carry coal by myself, but I do not have a cart," said Doctor's Nesthäkchen sheepishly.

"You're always nice to our Mäxchen, so I give you advice. Borrow one," directed the man when he saw the sad face of Annemarie. "Alone you cannot pull the heavy cart, it is too unstable. Where is your brother? He can help. The distinguished young gentleman must see what it is to have calluses on his hands." With that Kulicke hoisted his load onto his back.

Klaus, yes, Klaus had to come with her to Nordhafen. He had the strength. He must help get coal for Grandma.

"Hanne, how's Mom today?" Annemarie breathlessly blurted out; she had run up the two flights of stairs rapidly.

"Our lady is getting around, but…"

"Is Klaus here, Hanne? Call him."

"Yes, he's here. But I can't call him. That Klaus: yesterday evening he tied one on."

"Was he in the pub? Does he have a hangover?"

"Nope, he has the flu, a good case. And if you're here a long time, Annemiechen, you'll get sick." Hanne tried to keep her outside.

But Nesthäkchen wedged her foot in the door. "One moment, Hanne, is Hans here?"

"Nah, Annemiechen, he's already more than one hour in court. Our Hans is as diligent as his Papa. I have no time. We're a hospital. Three patients I have to care for. Over at the Thielens they have a nurse. Not here."

"You better not get sick, Hanne!"

"Me? What would I do then? You go back to Grandma, Annemiechen." The door flew shut.

Annemiechen did not go back to Grandma, but to the concierge apartment of Mr. Kulicke.

"What am I supposed to do, Mr. Kulicke? My brother Klaus is sick; he has the flu. My oldest brother is in court. Can I pull the cart alone?"

"Nah, you can't do that. I'll give you Mäxchen's stroller. You've seen it. You can haul 100 pounds of coal in it."

"Oh, dear Mr. Kulicke, that is kind of you." Annemarie blissfully held out to the caretaker her hand.

Kulicke brought out the shaky pram and described to Anne Marie how to get to Nordhafen. Then she set off with her carriage.

She passed by Vera's house. Hold on, Vera had to come along. The winter trip to northern Berlin was unappealing. But with her girlfriend, even freezing would be fun.

"It's fine that you visit me, Annemie," said Vera. "I was going to pick you up because today we have heat again."

"Three errors in two sets, Vera Burkhard, I can not possibly advance you from Lower Sixth." Annemarie glared over a nonexistent professorial pince-nez.

"You can give me a private lesson, Professor," laughed Vera.

"There is no time, Verachen. I have my stroller down the hallway and..."

"What do you have?" Vera laughed until tears filled her eyes. Annemie was funny! "A stroller you have down there? Which baby should it be for, you or me?"

"Both of us; I wish to undertake, like Cook and Nansen, a North Pole expedition. I want to ask you along."[48]

---

[48] Frederick Albert Cook (1865 – 1940) was an American explorer, physician, and ethnographer, noted for his claim of having reached the North Pole on April 21, 1908. Fridtjof Nansen (1861 – 1930) was a Norwegian explorer, scientist, diplomat, humanitarian and Nobel Peace Prize laureate. In his youth a champion skier and ice skater, he led the team that made the first crossing of the Greenland interior in 1888, and

"Annemie, we've frozen for the last two weeks. I do not need to travel to the North Pole," responded Vera jokingly.

"Never mind, you have to prove your friendship and come with me today." Annemarie's happy dimpled face looked serious. "I want to get coal for my grandma in the stroller, so she does not catch a cold and get sick."

"From the North Pole, Annemie?" Vera was puzzled. Was Annemarie joking or serious?

"Yes, of course, quickly get dressed. You have to dress warmly; it's pretty darn cold out there."

"From the North Pole you want to bring coals? Are you delirious, Annemie? Are you sick?" Fearfully, Vera looked at the cold red face of her friend. Did she have the flu?

"Nope, no, Verachen, I am quite healthy. You need not be so anxious. I'm going to Nordhafen, not the North Pole, although the North Pole may not be colder. At Nordhafen coal is sold from the ships, our porter told me. I want to bring a hundred pounds in the stroller for Grandma, and you will help me."

"Gladly, but my aunt is not home. I can not ask her permission."

---

won international fame after reaching a record northern latitude of 86°14' during his North Pole expedition of 1893–96.

"So much the better!" Annemarie rightly feared the objections that Vera's aunt would raise. "We'll move fast. When your aunt comes home, you'll be back."

A few minutes later, a blonde teenager and a black-haired teenager, peeping out with merry eyes from their enveloping fur coats, pushed an empty stroller through the snow glistening streets.

Tramp tramp tramp: their feet pounded the frozen snow to warm up. The road to Nordhafen was long. They passed the elegant apartment buildings of West Berlin, commercial buildings, then barracks-like workers' tenements. The people on the street changed. The girls saw no more precious furs, but threadbare coats and scarves, as the sharp northeast wind whistled.

The girls' eyes were no longer merry, but miserable. Weren't they at Nordhafen yet? The cold prickled their fingers that held the stroller handle.

"If we push the hundred pounds of coal home, we will be sweating," Annemarie consoled her freezing girlfriend. "Look, Vera, here come coal wagons, one, two, three. The coal supply is certainly not far off, "she exulted.

With renewed strength they went forward. At the next bend in the road, Nordhafen should lie before them. But what they saw was not exactly calculated to raise their sunken courage. The area in front of them was black with people and carts of all kinds swarming down to the boats from which the coal was unloaded. The hustle and cry could cause a newcomer to perish.

Vera held her courageous can-do girlfriend back anxiously.

"Are you going into that throng, truly, Annemie?" she asked hesitantly.

"Of course, you think we made the long journey in the cold to turn tail and run? You can wait here with the pram, Vera-chen. I'll see to obtaining some coal. Goodbye!" Annemarie in dark fur hat disappeared among all the people and horses' heads. Vera stood alone with her stroller, and tears sprang to her eyes. Was it cold or anxiety? A sharp wind whistled from the harbor. At the North Pole, it could not be as icy as here at Nordhafen. It was a painful sacrifice that Annemarie demanded of their friendship.

Fifteen minutes went by. Annemarie did not come back. Vera had absolutely no feeling in her hands and feet. With anxious eyes she watched the hands of a church clock. A quarter to twelve. She had to go home for dinner. She wanted this afternoon not to be late for school. Should she simply let go of the stroller and walk away? Such dark thoughts rolled blackly through Vera's head. The icy northeast wind had blown away warm feelings of friendship.

She felt something hot on her lips. Behind her stood Annemarie who held in her clammy fingers a pot of black hot coffee to Vera's mouth. "Drink this to warm up, Verachen. It is not mocha, but it is at least hot. I bought it over there in the still."

"Do you have coal?" The hot pot began to thaw Vera's frozen fingers. Her frozen feelings of friendship were reheated by Annemarie's loving care.

"Nope, not yet. It's too big a crowd. We could freeze here until tomorrow morning. But a cavalier I picked up will get me the coal." Annemarie pointed to a fifteen-year old boy following her. "He'll deliver the coal to Grandma. I gave him ten marks and promised him a warm meal and a pair of Klaus' discarded boots. He agreed. We can go home with the electric train. I leave the stroller."

"But the money for the coal? You can not give a strange man so much money, Annemie," warned Vera.

"I won't, you sly girl. He will accept payment on delivery. This afternoon we get our coal. Now we hurry home, otherwise Grandma will think I froze somewhere."

For better or worse, Annemarie wrote with numb fingers on a note pad the address of Grandma and handed it to her cavalier, who accepted it with a grin.

"The more coal, the better, and take good care of the stroller; it's not mine."

Doctor's smart Nesthäkchen rode home with Vera. Annemarie shivered with cold, but was proud she had done so fine a job.

Kulicke's stroller was never seen again. Doctor Braun had to pay a high price to replace it.

Grandma and Aunt Albertina got no coal, but Annemarie and Vera got the flu.

Chapter 13.
The Red-Capped

Two years passed since that nasty winter. Through the world a breath of Spring is felt. From Grunewald the breeze blows fragrantly and softly on the sea of stone houses in the metropolis. Golden waves of spring sunlight flow through the wide open windows into the rooms and hearts of men and women. Amidst the first snowdrops, in the streets and squares withered old hands offer to passers by violets for sale. Children whip about. Swallows twitter in the blue spring air.

What relief for humanity after an anxious winter. Spring has arrived! All seriousness, all oppressive thoughts are laughed away by golden sun.

Oh! Has the young child of man, with blond head buried on the dainty desk deep in books and notebooks, looked through her window at throbbing spring? Does she feel the sun caressing her fingers with its warm rays?

No, Doctor's Nesthäkchen, mumbling Latin words to herself, calculates with x-squared and y. Her pretty head is filled with historical numbers, data from literature, English and French verbs engaged in a colorful dance. Annemarie Braun has no time to listen to the first timid rustlings of spring. Still, the pressure, the iron tongs clutching her young soul, the weeks of torture are not over. In front of her stands the threat, the incessantly approaching specter: the final examination.

Oh God! Annemarie was for days no longer a human being, only an exam buffalo. This honorary title came naturally from Klaus, who according to his own famous dictum strongly discouraged his sister from touching a book. "The less you cram for exams, the better you do. Learning makes you stupid. Common sense rusts you."

But Annemarie had little confidence in the aphorisms of the lazy student. She remained devoted to Hans, who daily took the time to review with his sister one hour of Latin and mathematics. She had sweated through written class work. "I have messed up in Latin, Hänschen. I will be disgusting in the oral exams."

The dreadful day was imminent, tomorrow morning, about this time! She would either wear proudly the red graduate's cap, or, more likely, drums and trumpets would rattle resoundingly.

Did Margot Thielen at the opposite window have it any better? The exam approaching tomorrow pressed at Annemarie's heart with a thousand torments. The cozy girl sitting over there sketched graceful forms for book decoration, furniture fabrics and handicrafts, because she attended the School of Applied Arts.

Annemarie envied Vera Burkhard. As she had two years ago, Annemarie had regrets that Vera, who had not advanced, had to leave school. She secretly scolded Vera's uncle, a "tyrant." He had made a merciless end of their daily gatherings.

And today? What did Annemarie think about Uncle today? Intelligently and insightfully Government Councillor von Hohenfeld had acted: He let Vera learn artistic photography in a printing house and did not expose her to the exam demands of tomorrow.

There in the closet hung the new exam gown, dark, of course, in accord with the gloomy seriousness of the day. Mommy had no idea that it should see daylight tomorrow. Mom and Dad should not be upset and worry about their Lotte. There was time enough when she flunked.

Did Mommy actually know nothing? The door leading to the living room was opened softly. Muffled steps came closer. Worried mother's eyes caressed the pretty pale girl's face. Then a soft, tender hand touched flickering blonde hair; was it the hand of Mother or a finger of sun caressing her? The door closed again silently. A large piece of chocolate on the Latin dictionary was evidence of maternal concern. The daughter did not look up from her books.

Inside the next room, Mrs. Braun sighed to her husband: "If only Lotte's exams were over, either way. To me it's all the same. She shouldn't be bending over those books. The poor thing is pale from excitement and studying well into the night."

"It has gone on a long time, Elsbeth," said Dr. Braun. "If I had known beforehand that the girl would be consumed by it, I would never have given my consent. I thought our youngest, with her bold nature, would cope easily with the exam. But she looks to me like she has turned into a nervous young lady. The best thing about her, her healthy freshness of body and mind, has left her!"

On the windowsill, before the white desk, a beam of sunlight shot over a swallow. "Chirp chirp, Come on, Come on," it peeped enticingly. Annemarie did not notice.

From the opposite window came the friendship whistle, three times in quick succession, and penetrated the room. Annemarie, entrenched behind mathematical formulas, absently lifted her blond head.

At the window, Margot gestured in sign language. "I'm going to play tennis," proclaiming with finger contortions, "Come along! You will be fresher tomorrow than if you keep working today."

Anne Marie's forefinger was short and expressive in its response. She tapped it against her forehead. Her friend Margot was not consoling her, calling on her the day before the exam to play tennis. Then Annemarie's blond head dipped back into a sea of numbers and letters.

The telephone rang. Annemarie had given up the phone during the last weeks of work, so as not to be disturbed. Hanne's broad face peered through the door.

"Annemiechen, come to the phone."

"That's cuckoo, I have no time."

"I said that to Miss Vera, but she says she must speak to you."

"I'll come right away," the otherwise amiable Annemarie cried indignantly. She had become nervous and feverishly, fearfully excited after strenuous study for tomorrow's exam.

"When this crazy exam is over, I will make three crosses behind you," muttered Hanne grimly.

"Nah, Hanne, there's another job for you to do. You need to bake and cook for our graduates, if, yes, if the devil does not take me by my tail feathers." That was again Doctor's funny Nesthäkchen!

"Verachen, it's you" rang a moment later on the telephone. "How am I doing? Like a condemned man shortly before his execution. No, my heart, I can not go for a walk with you today! I will learn nothing more today? Well, at least I will need to make no recriminations if things go wrong. You'll call back to-morrow? Pinch both thumbs that all good spirits are merciful to me!"

Sunshine and springtime flourished outdoors, indoors pen scratching and the rush of pages turning. Annemarie slammed the physics book she was studying with a loud bang.

"That's enough!" said a voice behind Annemarie. "Today you're through working like an ox. Get dressed, we're going to the zoo."

"No, Hans, I still have an awful lot to review: Physics, the pretender to the throne, the Swabian poet school, Latin, and Milton's *Paradise Lost*. I won't be finished before midnight."

"And then you want to march fresh into the morning ex-am, little one? Not a chance. What you do not know today, you won't absorb in the next few hours. Now we go for a walk. Then you eat supper and put yourself to bed at half past nine. It is important that you have a clear, clear head at the exam. You'll never make it with sheer stored-up junk closet wisdom. Hear me, moss-covered head, get your hat, march!"

Annemarie wavered, "Only if you promise to interrogate me, Hänschen, in Latin and mathematics."

"The Devil if I shall! Not a word will be spoken while walk-ing away from the pesky exam. Come on, kid!"

"If I flunk, you are to blame, Hans!" Reluctantly Annemarie took her hat and jacket. She touched the examination gown hanging in the closet. Like a dagger, the feel of the gown drove through her heart. Oh God, it was reckless to leave the books in the lurch!

Doctor's Nesthäkchen had become a young lady in the last two years, hardly smaller than her brother, slim and slender as a willow branch. The blonde hair shimmering in the sunshine and the narrow face had become so dear and sweet that many admiring glances were cast upon the attractive girl. Annemarie did not notice. She was in her thoughts in the middle of tomorrow's exam.

She saw the school board sitting in front of her, foremost the principal. Her memory of her ill starred student council was still green. Miss Neubert's owl eye glasses sparkled viciously in sunlight and..."

"Annemie, isn't it pretty here?" Hans had stopped on the square beside the art school, in front of which was an expansive bed of colorful hyacinths and tulips.

"What do you mean?" Nesthäkchen looked but saw and heard nothing.

"Benighted lass, you've surely plugged up again between A and B square. Don't you think it would be interesting for me to walk in company where the fish is still talkative?" grumbled Brother kindly.

"I told you to leave me at home. The exam Furies are following me. I can not escape them."

"*Erinyes* you mean."[49]

Nesthäkchen laughed, brightly and youthfully, as she so gladly did. And it was as if the fresh laughter blew her soul free of the infernal pressure. Free and easy, Annemarie suddenly felt. Her golden sunny feet jumped back and forth. The shrubs wore light green jewels, and the trees were adorned with russet buds. Spring it was!

"Look, the young ducklings, how cute! The old one looks like Miss Drehmann. She waddles like that. If we do not break our necks in the exam, I must say to Ilse Hermann that she should do a little waddle at our festival to imitate Miss Drehmann." Hans no longer needed to complain of his silent companion. Annemarie's mouth was brought up to full speed.

"Are we insolent, Hänschen? As we sit down and study hard, we ridicule our proficient teachers. We are tentatively still

---

[49] In Greek mythology the Erinyes, also known as Furies, were female deities of vengeance; they were sometimes referred to as "infernal goddesses."

in their clutches. But the high school festival should occur tomorrow. If only we can get there in one piece."

On the *Neuer See,* Klaus pushed his sparkling skiff through the spring green, splashing it out from the shore. "Always clean, ladies and gentlemen," he exclaimed to his brother and sister.

Hans and Annemarie did not need to be asked twice. "Annemie can row. Physical application of force is the best antidote for spiritual power wastage," Klaus ordered.

Working out her muscles did wonders for Annemarie. The lake rippled gold-green between trickling twigs. Fish were playing in the clear water, which drew in the skiff. The specter of tomorrow sank to the lake bottom in the evening peace.

As the little ship docked at the boat house an hour later, Doctor's Nesthäkchen came as if from another world. Annemarie never would have thought it possible: she had not ruminated on tomorrow's exams during the whole time.

Of course, at home, as the faithless abandoned textbooks looked so reproachfully over the desk, she felt quite guilty. But at dinner, it was necessary to appear as relaxed as possible, so her parents would not smell a rat. The oars had flushed her cheeks and stimulated her appetite. She had choked at noon on every bite. Now she feasted bravely. Father and Mother were happy that the food tasted good to their youngest.

A long, anxious night lay before her. Would it have been better if she had sat until dawn at her books, instead of sleeplessly wallowing on her pillow? Annemarie did not have much time to ask this question. She forgot that rowing not only reddens the cheeks and increases the appetite. The unaccustomed muscular exertion makes you really tired. Doctor's Nesthäkchen had believed that all night she would not be able to close her eyes. But gentle, sweet sleep shielded her from the evil exam day.

Oh, if she would never wake up! What's that feeling when you wake up happy and clear eyed the morning, yet have a dark, unconscious sensation: there was something bad and oppressive. What was it? And then fright burns like a whip: exam day! The dreaded day has arrived! You can not hide from it. It is here and brings merciless horrors and miseries. Could one do nothing to escape its clutches? Oh, yes, you could call in sick. Actually, she was sick: quite ill she felt. Her aching temples throbbed like liquid fire. If you were sick, you did not have to enter the auditorium, the one whose immense interior, in its unaccustomed emptiness, was like an gaping maw, ready to devour the poor victims. You did not need to stand before the piercing eyes of the council or impaling looks of the teaching staff. You could remain quietly at home in bed, drink some peppermint tea, and flunk out. Lovely! Out of the question.

Thus ended Doctor's Nesthäkchen's thoughts of escape as she jumped out of bed.

The new exam dress: in her childish vanity she had been pleased with it. Now she felt a horror of it. How solemn it looked. As if she should go to her own funeral. Textbooks: she did not need them today. But she had to clear the books away all the same; otherwise Mommy would be suspicious. Before Mommy got up, Nesthäkchen must be over the mountains.

Klaus, otherwise not a morning person, drove the exam jitters from his sister's pen. "So, you've put on your execution uniform, Annemie," he giggled as he tried to cheer her up.

"Oh, Klaus, can not the poor sinner feel peace in her last hours. I think the gallows would be a treat compared to exam day." Indeed, Nesthäkchen looked like she was going to her execution.

"You can put paper cribs in your sleeve, Annemie, a fine record of names and data that you did not get into your head."

"Nope. I have half sleeves in the new dress. But I have disguised a paper napkin as a handkerchief; everything is on it that I do not know. If the school board asks me something, I will have to blow my nose first." Annemarie had to laugh at her own gallows humor.

"That's right, Annemie, you're solidly on top of things," praised her brother. "And do not let yourself be intimidated. Respond arrogantly, whether you know the answer or not. Mostly, they do not hear you."

"Hans, don't give me any bread. I can't swallow a bite. I feel quite miserable looking at it."

"Don't become a hysterical female, Annemie. Here, sit down and have breakfast." Hans squeezed into an adjacent chair and stood guard to see that his sister drank her cocoa and ate her bread.

She got it down. Annemarie had not thought it possible.

She had to leave quickly. She didn't want Mom to catch her in the examination dress.

"Do your job well, Annemie. The calmer you are, the more clearly you will be able to answer all questions. Do not worry, you've learned something."

Hans was reassuring. He loosened the tongs that compressed her chest.

Father appeared at the breakfast table. He threw a searching look at his moping Nesthäkchen. But he did his Lotte a favor and said nothing. He patted her pale cheek encouragingly.

"Break a leg," Klaus whispered to her lovingly in the corridor.

"For shame, Klaus!"

"That is the best blessing for exams. Since you can say to each student, tonight I'll take you to the pub."

"First I have to back out of the jaws of hell."

Hanne stuck her head out of the kitchen. "Hush Annemiechen, here are extra sandwiches. Food will not make you stupid. I see that you hardly eat today. Don't be frightened. You have learned more than all the professors put together. Once you plop down there, you can recite them the unvarnished truth."

Annemie had to laugh: the faithful Hanne in her Berlin brazenness wanted the student to lecture to the Professors.

Puck accompanied Annemarie to the stairs, as if the clever animal noticed that his young friend was undergoing an ordeal.

"Down to joy." Doctor's Nesthäkchen descended the stairs.

At the doorstep stood Vera and Margot, the two faithful friends. "Today we didn't want you to go alone to school."

"We want to escort you."

"You probably think you're paying your last respects." Annemarie pressed her girlfriends' hands gratefully. "Children, you've got it good. You do not have to go to the scaffold."

Bright spring sun poured from heaven. Gray rainy weather would have corresponded more to Annemarie's state of mind. The girlfriends were talking animatedly from both sides in order to distract Nesthäkchen from the impending horrors.

Annemarie barely heard them. She walked as if in a dream-like state. But it was a bad dream, a nightmare, crouching on her chest and clenching her throat.

"Annemie, watch out." Margot grabbed her arm.

"In a hair you would have been under that car!"

"I would have been more comfortable than I am now."

The red brick building, the Schubert Lyceum, appeared in front of them.

"God protect you, Annemie. In the break at twelve I come to get you." Vera kissed her tenderly.

"Good luck, Annemie!"

"Don't wish me luck, Margot, otherwise it will definitely go wrong. Oh, if I were already out of there!"

A breathless silence reigned in the corridors. On the school exam day honor hung in the balance. Here it was, the day of reckoning, the key part of life, school, over and done. Some girls were pressed to the heart, most jolly and carefree. Was Doctor's Nesthäkchen walking the familiar hallway for the last time? Or would she be forced to remain a schoolgirl?

The high school graduates were gathered in the upper sixth, all with colorless faces and frightened eyes, ten in number. "Like a flock of sheep in a thunderstorm," thought Annemarie. She surprised herself that she could think this way in these anxious minutes.

The lower section of the upper sixth students unpacked red caps, ten in number. Would every cap find her owner? The red was burning their eyes. Marlene felt almost a physical pain when she looked at the caps. She passed her ice cold hand to Annemarie.

"In mathematics I will easily fail."

"I'll flunk Latin, Marlene. Do not get so terribly agitated. Hans says, the calmer you are, the better your chances." Doctor's Nesthäkchen assuaged her girlfriend all too well, while flying to pieces herself.

Ilse Hermann's long blond braids no longer hung down her back; they were fashioned into a bun. Ilse babbled on and on, numbers and names to herself. Marianne armed herself against the risk of eating a piece of cheese bread. She claimed, in her excitement, to be entirely without appetite.

The girls' teacher, Professor Möbus, entered the classroom.

"Well, ladies, you're not scared? No deathly pale faces? Do not act as though you have landed in the cannibal isles. We don't scalp anyone who has learned something.

"Yes, if you have learned something." Each was convinced at this moment of her complete ignorance, despite the extensive teaching that had been funneled into her head.

"However, I can not deny," continued the professor, "that three of you will not take the exam."

Ten hearts beat in sudden fright. None of the terrified chicks saw how comically Doctor Möbus squinted over his glasses. "Miss Ulrich, don't learn anything more, it will not benefit you."

Oh, Marlene knew that she had totally botched her math work. At the end she was not called to take an exam. Who were the poorest students, the three? The professor knew beforehand that they would not pass the exam. Every single girl thought, in her excitement, that the teacher was looking at her.

"Time and the hour runs through the roughest day." They had learned the words of Shakespeare. But the meaning had not occurred to the carefree young things. Today it did. The most frightful minutes finally passed.

"Ladies, you can go to the auditorium!" There they were: the terrifying words.

With trembling knees the girls obeyed.

Marlene and Ilse went hand in hand. Annemarie Braun was ahead of them. Now that the time had come, she did not want to let on how miserable she felt. Miss Neubert's owl's eyes should not gloat over her weakness.

They sat at a long table next to each other, all who had passed through the long lower secondary school years. In the middle the school councillor was enthroned. Actually he looked quite human, the old gentleman. He laughed in concert with the Principal. How could the men laugh while ten young souls writhed in agony? At least the councillor and the principal were in good spirits.

The professor read the names of the high school graduates. They answered with a tense *here*.

The principal unfolded solemnly a white document. "The following have passed the written final examination..." There was again the reading of ten names.

God be drummed and piped. Nobody flunked the written exam.

"For oral exam will be admitted..."

Seven names: Annemarie and Marlene's were not among them.

Marlene's bloodshot eyes were hot. Annemarie clenched her fingers together. She did not want to perform a drama for Owl Eyes.

"From the oral exam will be excused, on the basis of a pass of the written exam: Miss Annemarie Braun"

"Hurrah!"

Like a lark, cheers rose in the sober auditorium! What had the impulsive Annemarie asked of the council or of Owl Eyes? She was freed from the oral exam. Hurray!

"Miss Elli Jordan and Miss Marlene Ulrich," the director continued his interrupted speech, smiling.

"Marlenchen!" Unabashedly spinning in blissful happiness, Annemarie wrapped her arm around her friend. That was good, because Marlene's knees were buckling . The sudden joy after the constant fear overwhelmed the delicate nervous system of the young girl. Helping hands gave her a glass of water.

"Ladies, you can leave the auditorium. I speak on behalf of the teaching staff and offer all best wishes," said the principal, turning once more to the three lucky ones.

Bows. Miss Herring pressed Annemarie's hand as she passed by. Owl Eyes, Miss Neubert, looked strangely friendly. Marianne Davis cast a painful glance at Annemarie. Then the door of the dreaded auditorium shut behind them. The jaws of hell had spewed them out unharmed.

Outside rang a "Hurrah!" from the throats of the lower section of the upper sixth. Red hats were waved in wild joy. The red hat, the badge of dignity of the new graduates, rested on Doctor's Nesthäkchen's curly blond hair.

»Children, I am blessed" The red hatted Annemarie swirled in impetuous exuberance. Elli Jordan, a quiet, hardworking girl, was running around in circles! "Marlenchen, so you totally botched math? You say nothing. Are you deprived of the joy of language?"

Marlene's pale face was gradually assuming its normal color.

"Oh, Annemarie, I can not rejoice as loudly as you. I have to rejoice quietly. And one more thing: The poor Ilse! She's probably doing badly. I have to constantly think of Ilse. I have transgressed. I feel that I left her."

"Go back inside and tell the school board, if my inseparable cousin has not been exempted from the Oral, I won't eat. You've got a mouth, Marlene!"

The third "Hurrah!" was loud. It was for the huge cake provided for the lower section. One piece after another was consumed. The healthy young appetites, on strike for days, had returned with a vengeance.

"I must hurry home to report the good news. At the twelve o'clock break we meet again. Hopefully the seven will not suffer shipwreck. Mr. Piefke, we are through, freed from the Oral." Anne Marie's bright voice gave the janitor, in his little garden house, a terrible fright.

"I do congratulate you, kindest Miss. I knew yesterday but it was an official secret." Piefke had a certain nobility about him, but accepted graciously the five marks that each of the outgoing girls thrust into his hand.

Arm in arm, the red-capped girls traversed the busy streets of Berlin. Annemarie, mobile as mercury, jumped and danced along, as if she were not a grownup young lady who sat for the last time at school, but Doctor's Nesthäkchen who had to be tamed by school discipline. Every passerby, even the grumpiest curmudgeon, had a warm feeling when he looked into the radiant young eyes.

At a canter she went up the stairs at home, two at a time.

"Hanne I'm through!"

"The uncles will get it from me if they're crazy enough to flunk our child who studied day and night."

Anne Marie's mischievous laughter interrupted the cursing Hanne.

"But, Hanne, I didn't flunk. I'm through, finished, no oral exam because I got an "A" on the written. Oh, there's mom."

Anne Marie, a laughing, sobbing mess, was at the neck of her mother!

"Mommy, cruelty to animals is over! I have been excused from the oral, Marlene Ulrich also. Oh, Mommy, I'm so happy!" Mother held her youngest in her arms.

"My Lotte!" she said softly, because a mother is worried about her child more than herself. Had she not long since discovered that the exam dress was missing from the cupboard?

Klaus, who had used the worthy event to skip college today, came forward joyfully. "Did I not I tell you, Annemie, fools have the most luck? What have you been all of your life? A buffalo. If a man has pig, he also comes through life."

"I would not depend on it, my son. Hard work is a more secure guarantee," Mother said. And Puck, who circled Annemarie wildly, vigorously barked his objection to Klaus.

"Is father at home, and Hans?" Annemarie was eager to proclaim her luck.

No, father was already in his practice and Hans in the lawyer's office. Why was the telephone here? On all sides everyone shouted into the electric wire that Doctor's Nesthäkchen graduated with distinction and was excused from the oral.

Father interrupted his patient care to press his Lotte quickly to his heart. "I get soon my little assistant. The first step is made. It's about time!"

Grandma appeared with beaming pride and an auspicious giant candy dish. She had guessed that Nesthäkchen would pass the exam with distinction; actually, she had known it in advance. Aunt Albertina came with happily dangling curls, Vera with many kisses, and brother Hans gallantly with roses. Nesthäkchen was at the center of the doctor's house.

Amidst the bliss nobody forgot the seven poor victims who were stewing in the hellfire of the exam. In time for the twelve o'clock recess, Annemarie came back to school to hear how things stood with the others.

The oral went well. The School Board and Principal were hugely nice and lobbed easy questions. "If it does not get worse, we all get through," said Ilse relieved to her intimate, Marlene, while Marianne devoured one piece of cake after another to strengthen herself.

Yes, all came through it.

The next night the colorful lanterns with garlands and a fairy-like appearance adorned the gym above the ten lucky red-capped girls. They sat at long tables, teaching staff and students, otherwise strictly separated by the wall of respectful discipline, today joyfully together. Everyone tasted Hanne's Italian salad, and they feasted on rolls and pies in unending profusion. They sang brazenly and boldly around the peach punch bowl satirical songs about school and teachers. And no one could give anyone a demerit; even Owl Eyes was a no longer a threat. Oh blessed, golden freedom!

The gym, which was actually for all school classes, permitted some revelry; but finally looked disapprovingly at the boisterous crowd of girls, as a drama was staged.

"The Holy Court" it was called. The author, Annemarie Brown, wanted Miss Neubert to prove what she had learned. Five black masked figures, eerie black larval masks before their merry faces, sat at the stroke of midnight in judgment on the poor teachers.

With somber voice and punitive hands raised they shouted their sepulchral "Woe! Alas! Woe!"

"None of the victims was pardoned. Everyone had sinned in the long years of teaching and was ruthlessly dismissed and condemned by the holy court. Miss Neubert was, because of insuperable aversion to bakeries, turned into an owl. Woe! Woe! Woe!

Annemarie Braun made her drama a bit too colorful. Not just some worthy teacher, but the gym shook her aged head. The swinging rings and parallel bars clinked softly. However, most teachers put a good face on the bad game and laughed with the lasses. Professor Herwig, due to his difficult Latin exam, was sentenced to have his snuffbox withdrawn. He did not consent until the young dramatist had taken a pinch of punishment from the selfsame box. Instead of Woe! Woe! Woe! resounded Achoo! Achoo! Achoo!

Piefke got the piano from the singing class and everyone danced. Fidelitas began, at the teachers' recommendation.[50] Tomorrow was no Day of Freedom for them, but an ordinary school day.

---

[50] In Fidelitas, players take on the role of faithful citizens in a medieval city exerting influence in order to gain the credibility needed to lead the charge against the corrupt crown.

Instead of their brothers and cousins in the sanctuary of the girls' school, the graduates pounced on the leftover buns and cakes and whirled, despite all disapproving head shakes of the Gymnasium, among ladders, bars and swinging rings.

Floor lamps that looked like fireflies attracted the red-capped girls, singing as they exited the walls of the school into a new life.

May it bring you luck, Nesthäkchen!

Figure 8. The next night the colorful lanterns with garlands and a fairy-like appearance adorned the gym above the ten lucky red-capped girls.

Epilogue

As Else Ury begins her story in this volume, a German corporal, Adolf Hitler, who had been blinded by gas attack, October 14, 1918, lay in a military hospital in Pasewalk, a Pomeranian town 138 km NE of Berlin. According to a comrade, Hans Mend, Hitler was given to discourse on the dismal state of morale and dedication to the cause on the home front in Germany: "He sat in the corner of our mess holding his head between his hands in deep contemplation. Suddenly he would leap up, and running about excitedly, say that in spite of our heavy guns victory would be denied us, for the invisible foes of the German people were a greater danger than the biggest cannon of the enemy."

The eye injury in October put an end to Hitler's service in World War I. He learned of the German surrender while recovering at Pasewalk. Infuriated and frustrated by the news—"I staggered and stumbled back to my ward and buried my aching head between the blankets and pillow"—Hitler was certain the German people, the Jews in particular, had betrayed both him and his fellow soldiers with a *Dolchstoß,* a stab in the back. In

1941, Hitler as Führer would reveal the degree to which his career and its awful legacy had been shaped by the First World War. He wrote, "I brought home with me my experiences at the front; out of them I built my National Socialist community" and the gas chambers, where his willing helpers murdered Else Ury, her younger sister Käthe, and millions of other Jews.

Bibliography

- Brech, Sarah Maria. Als Deutsche "Nesthäkchens" Mutter ermordeten. Die Zeit 13 Jan 2013.
- Brentzel, Marianne. Mir kann doch nichts geschehen ...: Das Leben der Nesthäkchen-Autorin Else Ury. Ebersbach & Simon (March 13, 2015).
- Bullock, Alan. Hitler: A Study in Tyranny. Harper & Row 1964 p 53.
- Kershaw, Ian. Hitler: 1889-1936 Hubris. W. W. Norton & Company (April 17, 2000) pp 97-120.
- Lehrer, Steven (2000). Wannsee House and the Holocaust. McFarland & Company. p. 104. ISBN 978-0-7864-0792-7.
- Lüke, Martina. "Else Ury – A Representative of the German-Jewish Bürgertum. Not an Essence but a Positioning": German-Jewish Women Writers 1900-38. Eds. Godela Weiss-Sussex and Andrea Hammel. Martin Meidenbauer Verlag: München, 2009 and Institute of Germanic & Romance Studies; School of Advanced Study, University of London, 2009 (Publication of the Institute of Germanic Studies, 93). 77-93.
- Mazon, Patricia M. Gender and the Modern Research University: The Admission of Women to German Higher Education, 1865–1914. Stanford University Press; 1 edition (August 4, 2003) pp 166-175.

- Pech, Klaus-Ulrich: Ein Nesthaken als Klassiker. Else Urys Nesthäkchen-Reihe. In: Klassiker der Kinder- und Jugendliteratur. Edited by Bettina Hurrelmann. Fischer Verlag. Frankfurt/M. 1995, pp 339 – 357
- Redmann, Jennifer. Nostalgia and Optimism in Else Ury's "Nesthäkchen" Books for Young Girls in the Weimar Republic. The German Quarterly, Vol. 79, No. 4 (Fall, 2006), pp. 465-483.

Proof

Made in the USA
Charleston, SC
13 February 2016